There was silence f[...]
there was a problem[...]
Rose asked, "And so [...]
too young to actually [...]

Defying all laws of inertia, the acceleration of Kennedy's heart rate crashed to a halt like a car plowing into a brick wall. "What do you mean?"

"Like, what if you're too young but you still get pregnant?"

"How young?" Kennedy spoke both words clearly and slowly, as if rushing might drive the timid voice away for good.

"Like thirteen."

Praise for *Unplanned*
by Alana Terry

"Deals with **one of the most difficult situations a pregnancy center could ever face**. The message is **powerful** and the story-telling **compelling**." ~ William Donovan, *Executive Director Anchorage Community Pregnancy Center*

"Alana Terry does an amazing job tackling a very **sensitive subject from the mother's perspective**." ~ Pamela McDonald, *Director Okanogan CareNet Pregnancy Center*

"**Thought-provoking** and intense ... Shows **different sides of the abortion argument**." ~ Sharee Stover, *Wordy Nerdy*

"Alana has a way of sharing the gospel **without being preachy**." ~ Phyllis Sather, *Purposeful Planning*

She wouldn't be victimized again. She had to get away. She wouldn't let him catch up to her. A footstep on the concrete. Not a fabrication. Not this time. It was real. Real as the scientific method. Real as her parents' love for her. Real as death. In the pitch darkness, she rushed ahead, running her fingers along the grimy wall so she would know which way to go as she sprinted down the walkway. What did contracting a few germs compare to getting murdered?

How close was he now? And why couldn't she have remembered her pepper spray? She strained her ears but only heard the slap of her boots on the walkway, the sound of her own panting, the pounding of her heart valves in her pericardial sac. She didn't want to stop, couldn't slow down, but she had to save her strength. She needed energy to fight back when he caught up. She couldn't hear him, but that didn't mean he wasn't coming.

Any second now.

Praise for *Paralyzed*
by Alana Terry

"Alana Terry has **done the almost unthinkable**; she has written a story with **raw emotions of real people**, not the usual glossy Christian image." ~ Jasmine Augustine, Tell Tale Book Reviews

"Alana has a way of **using fiction to open difficult issues** and make you think." ~ Phyllis Sather, Author of *Purposeful Planning*

"Once again, Ms. Terry brings a **sensitive but important issue to the forefront** without giving an answer. She **leaves it up to the reader** to think about and decide." ~ Darla Meyer, Book Reviewer

Without warning, the officer punched Reuben in the gut. Reuben doubled over as the cop brought his knee up to his face. Reuben staggered.

"You dirty n—." Without warning, the cop whipped out his pistol and smashed its butt against Reuben's head. He crumpled to the ground, where the officer's boots were ready to meet him with several well-placed kicks.

Throwing all rational thoughts aside, Kennedy jumped on his back. Anything to get him to stop beating Reuben. The officer swore and swatted at her. Kennedy heard herself screaming but had no idea what she was saying. She couldn't see anything else, nor could she understand how it was that when her normal vision returned, she was lying on her back, but the officer and Reuben were nowhere to be seen.

Praise for *Policed*
by Alana Terry

"*Policed* could be taken **from the headlines of today's news**." ~ Meagan Myhren-Bennett, *Blooming with Books*

"**A provocative story** with authentic characters." ~ Sheila McIntyre, *Book Reviewer*

"It is important for Christian novelists to address today's issues like police misconduct and racism. Too often writers tiptoe around **serious issues faced by society**." ~ Wesley Harris, *Law Enforcement Veteran*

"Focuses on a prevalent issue in today's society. Alana **pushes the boundaries more than any other Christian writer**." ~ Angie Stormer, *Readaholic Zone*

Wayne Abernathy, the Massachusetts state senator, was towering over a teenage boy who sat crumpled over the Lindgrens' dining room table.

"I don't care what you have to do to fix him," Wayne blasted at Carl.

Kennedy froze. Nobody heard her enter. Carl sat with his back to her, but she could still read the exhaustion in his posture.

Wayne brought his finger inches from the boy's nose. "Do whatever you have to do, Pastor. Either straighten him up, or so help me, he's got to find some other place to live."

Kennedy bit her lip, trying to decide if it would be more awkward to leave, make her presence known, or stay absolutely still.

Wayne's forehead beaded with sweat, and his voice quivered with conviction. "It's impossible for any son of mine to turn out gay."

Praise for *Straightened*
by Alana Terry

"Alana doesn't take a side, but she makes you really think. She **presents both sides of the argument in a very well written way**." ~ Diane Higgins, *The Book Club Network*

"No matter what conviction you have on the subject, I'm fairly certain **you will find that this novel has a character who accurately represents that viewpoint**." ~ Justin, Avid Reader

"Alana Terry doesn't beat up her readers, but, rather she gets them to either examine their own beliefs or encourages them to **find out for themselves what they believe and what the Bible says**." ~ Jasmine Augustine, *Tell Tale Book Reviews*

She shook her head. "I don't know. I can't say. I just know that something is wrong here. It's not safe." She clenched his arm with white knuckles. "Please, I can't ... We have to ..." She bit her lip.

He frowned and let out a heavy sigh. "You're absolutely certain?"

She nodded faintly. "I think so."

"It's probably just nerves. It's been a hard week for all of us." There was a hopefulness in his voice but resignation in his eyes.

She sucked in her breath. "This is different. Please." She drew her son closer to her and lowered her voice. "For the children."

"All right." He unbuckled his seatbelt and signaled one of the flight attendants. "I'm so sorry to cause a problem," he told her when she arrived in the aisle, "but you need to get my family off this plane. Immediately."

Praise for *Turbulence*
by Alana Terry

"This book is **hard to put down** and is a **suspenseful roller coaster of twists and turns**." ~ Karen Brooks, *The Book Club Network*

"I've enjoyed all of the Kennedy Stern novels so far, but **this one got to me in a more personal way** than the others have." ~ *Fiction Aficionado*

"I love that the author is **not afraid to deal with tough issues all believers deal with**." ~ Kit Hackett, *YWAM Missionary*

Infected

a novel by Alana Terry

Note: The views of the characters in this novel do not necessarily reflect the views of the author, nor is their behavior necessarily condoned.

The characters in this book are fictional. Any resemblance to real persons is coincidental. No part of this book may be reproduced in any form (electronic, audio, print, film, etc.) without the author's written consent.

Infected
Copyright © 2017 Alana Terry
ISBN 978-1-941735-32-9
May, 2017

Cover design by Damonza.

www.alanaterry.com

"Praise the Lord, my soul; all my inmost being, praise his holy name. Praise the Lord, my soul, and forget not all his benefits— who forgives all your sins and heals all your diseases."

Psalm 103:1-3

CHAPTER 1

So I sing because I'm happy,
And I sing because I'm free.
His eye is on the sparrow,
And I know he watches me.

Kennedy groaned when her phone screeched at her. She knew who was calling, and she knew exactly what he'd have to say.

"Hey, Dad."

"You've been following this thing on Channel 2?" His voice was breathless. Panicked.

Just like she expected.

"Yeah, I've been keeping track." She hadn't logged onto any news outlets since breakfast that morning. Checking in with reality once a day was enough for her.

"Ok, because this isn't just something you can ignore, Kensie girl. That's what you like to do. But this is too serious."

1

"I know, Dad." Did he forget they'd had this exact same conversation twenty-four hours ago?

"So tell me what precautions you're taking. What will you be doing for spring break?"

She rolled her eyes, certain he could sense the gesture all the way from his printing office overseas. What time was it now in China anyway? Wasn't it the middle of the night? "I'm staying at the Lindgrens'." She'd told him her plans at least a dozen times by now. For someone who knew the name and origin of every little virus that reared its head in the developing world, her dad could be ridiculously forgetful.

"So Carl and Sandy are still taking that anniversary trip, are they?"

Kennedy moved the phone slightly away from her face to try to mask her annoyed sigh. "They're just driving a few hours away. And it's only for a night."

"They've already gone?"

"No, they're getting packed right now."

Even with the guest room door shut, Carl and Sandy's good-humored bickering hummed in Kennedy's one ear while her dad's fretting echoed in her other.

"I really don't get why they decided to go."

"Because it's their anniversary." At least now that she

was a college student and thousands of miles away in Massachusetts, she wouldn't get grounded for letting so much exasperation lace her voice. "Some folks do that sort of romantic stuff, you know."

"Not in the middle of an epidemic, they don't."

Kennedy glanced at her phone. They'd only been talking two minutes, and she was already sick of this conversation. What did her dad expect? For Carl and Sandy to put their entire life on hold because some people had come down with a bad infection? He might not know it from his little office in Yanji, but life was going on in spite of the fearmongering media. Passengers were still flying on planes. Children attending schools. Adults going to work, shopping for groceries, living their regular day-to-day lives. Maybe things were scarier for her dad way out there in Jilin Province, but here in the Boston area, there really wasn't anything to worry about. This was just the kind of news story that her dad loved to fixate on. Another way he tried to control her life from the other side of the world.

"Ok, so tell me what kind of safety measures you're taking. How are you going to make sure you're not exposing yourself to anyone who's possibly contaminated?"

Well, I'm not living in Bangladesh or near a herd of pigs, for one thing. Of course, that wasn't the answer her dad was

3

looking for. He didn't need a geography lesson about the virus's origins. He'd tracked the spread of the disease for weeks before the first confirmed cases arrived in the US, before the American public ever heard the words *Nipah virus*. But he was waiting for her answer, and unless she wanted him to find some germ-proof convent to lock her away in for the rest of her life, she had to appease his paranoia.

"I'm not going to shopping malls, airports, or any other places with crowds. I'm not eating out in any restaurants. I've got my Germ-X, and I'm using it regularly." Even without her dad's constant reminding, when did Kennedy ever forget her Germ-X? She was the most germophobic premed student at Harvard, an idiosyncrasy that her roommate loved to tease her about.

"So you'll be staying inside all day then? That's good. What about Carl and Sandy's son? Is he old enough to wash his hands on his own yet?"

"Yeah, Dad. He's in the third grade."

"Well, you should probably still do it for him. Especially before you eat any meals together. And don't cuddle much. Best to keep a safe distance."

"All right." She was only halfway listening now as she unpacked her clothes into the top drawer in the Lindgrens' guest room.

4

"What about social get-togethers? Do you have anyone you're planning to invite over while you're babysitting?"

Kennedy suspected her dad was subtly referring to her boyfriend Dominic. The only thing more annoying than listening in while her dad's crisis training kicked into high gear was talking to him about her love life, with all his awkward half-questions and insinuations. Last January, just two weeks after she'd officially started dating him, her dad actually asked about Dominic's opinion on birth control.

"How in the world should I know?" Kennedy had shouted.

Apparently, her reaction pleased her father.

It was funny to think of her dad worrying about her and her boyfriend. Dominic had told Kennedy very early on in their relationship that he and his deceased wife hadn't kissed until their wedding day. And he'd told her time and time again since then that he planned to take the same slow and steady approach in any future relationships he entered.

That was fine with Kennedy, at least mostly. No, it was totally fine. She didn't have time to be worried about that sort of stuff anyway. She and Dominic spent time together once a week on Sundays. He'd pick her up and take her to his cousin's home church. They'd go out for lunch after that, walk around Boston Common if the weather was nice, then

5

say good-bye. They talked every couple nights on the phone, sometimes quick check-in calls but sometimes deep conversations where Dominic would allude to the stress he was under at work or Kennedy would ask him some of the Bible questions she'd been storing up.

They didn't have a lot of time together, but it's not like she could have offered Dominic a lot more anyway. Kennedy was taking double science courses this year, organic chemistry as well as biology, each with their own lectures and weekly labs. To top it off, she'd enrolled in an MCAT prep course that met two nights a week. Part of her early acceptance into Harvard med school was contingent on her passing the entrance exam. After all the time and energy she'd put into her first two years of undergrad studies, she wasn't about to fail.

She shook her head and remembered her dad was waiting for her response. "No, nobody's coming over. At least nothing's planned." Should she mention that there was no way Dominic would come over to the Lindgrens' house, regardless of the time of day or night, without the assurance of at least two other adults present? Kennedy appreciated his commitment to purity, but sometimes she wondered what he was so afraid of. Did he think she'd turn into some sort of sex-crazed fiend and molest him the minute she found herself alone in a room with him?

"Ok, that's good. So basically, you're staying home all day then? Not going anywhere?"

"Well, I have to take Woong to school tomorrow morning and pick him up again at three. But other than that, there's nowhere else I have to be." She was glad Carl and Sandy would only be gone for one night. She still wasn't sure what she'd do to keep Woong entertained two afternoons by herself, but she'd come up with something. Woong had gotten a Wii for his birthday (a random date Carl and Sandy picked out of a calendar since the South Korean orphanage had no records of his birth), but Sandy was adamant that he couldn't play more than half an hour on school days, and then only once he'd finished his homework, his quiet reading time, and his afternoon chores.

Kennedy just hoped that when Sandy came home, she wouldn't be disappointed if she found the house a complete disaster. Kennedy had a hard time keeping her itty-bitty dorm room tidy. She had no idea how she'd keep up an entire house with a boy as rambunctious as Woong.

"So he's still going to school this week?" her dad asked, and Kennedy couldn't tell if his incredulous tone meant he wondered why all schools weren't on the same spring break schedule as Harvard's or why anyone would keep a Medford, Massachusetts elementary school open when a few unfortunate individuals across the state had found themselves fighting for their lives against some hitherto obscure Nipah virus.

"Yeah, there's still school."

Her dad whispered something under his breath. If Kennedy had to guess, it sounded most like *unbelievable*. She glanced at the time. Carl and Sandy were late.

"And what about groceries?" he asked. "Is there enough there or are you going to have to go shopping at all?"

Kennedy had only arrived at the Lindgrens' an hour earlier. How did he expect her to have the entire next thirty-six hours planned out?

"Sandy cooked a whole bunch of casseroles and stuff for us to heat up. There's enough food here to last a month," she told her dad.

He let out his breath. "Let's hope it doesn't come down to that."

CHAPTER 2

"All right, pumpkin, I showed you where the lasagna is, didn't I?" Sandy opened the fridge door absently and shut it again.

"Only about half a dozen times," Carl replied. He had two overnight bags strapped over his shoulders and kept trying to make his way to the door that led to the garage.

"Well, you know we're only going to be a few hours away. I gave you our schedule, right?"

"You printed it up and put a copy on the fridge, a copy in the bathroom, and a copy in the den. Don't you remember?" Carl tried to adjust his pants while carrying so much luggage.

"I just want to make sure I've covered it all. I'm certain I'm forgetting something."

"Like we need to check into the B&B in an hour and a half, and it's going to take us twice that long to get there?"

Sandy shook her head and frowned. "No, that's not it. I gave you the number for Woong's pediatrician, didn't I?"

Kennedy nodded, certain she'd find the number taped to the emergency contact list above the microwave if it weren't already on the three-page handwritten note Sandy had penned in her flowing cursive that sat folded in Kennedy's pocket.

"And I showed you where the car keys are hanging up by the garage door. Oh, that's something I should have mentioned. Nick might stop by to borrow the Honda. Since we're taking the van, I told him he could use the car whenever he needs."

"Yeah, no problem." Kennedy was just glad she wouldn't be the one driving the church's clunky, painted, hipster bus all over Massachusetts.

"Oh, that's another thing," Sandy went on. "Woong went to a birthday party last weekend, and he watched *Princess Bride*. It's put all kinds of fancy ideas in his head, but the rules are no sword fighting in the house. And you've got to watch him because I think he learned a bad word. I'm not entirely sure. So you listen out for that and tell me if you run into any problems."

Kennedy wondered how long ago it was that her own parents had worried about her picking up a bad word or two from a movie.

Sandy stared around the room. "So you know we won't

be home until late tomorrow night, right, love? Carl's taking me out to a fancy dinner on the Isabella. It's going to be so romantic."

"If we ever make it there," Carl grumbled.

"We're almost ready, honey, just you wait." She offered Kennedy an apologetic smile. "He's upset because I'm taking him to see the opera tonight. It was the deal we made. Tonight the opera, tomorrow the new action movie with that famous guy playing in it. You know the one I mean. He's in the movie with the lady, you know. The blonde one."

Carl rolled his eyes. "Can we go now?" He nudged their bags a little closer to the door. "Otherwise I'll have to stop and use the bathroom again."

"Already? I'm serious, honey, you really need to stop drinking so much water. It can't be good for your kidneys."

"Actually ..." Carl began, but Sandy cut him off.

"Hold on, let me remember. There's something I've got to tell Kennedy. Now what was it? You know Woong starts getting ready for bed at eight, right? It takes him quite a long time to settle down."

"I'm sure we'll be fine," Kennedy said, not feeling nearly as certain as she tried to sound.

Sandy took a step toward the door then spun around on

her heel. "Oh! That's what it was." She bustled past and pulled a piece of paper off the top of the microwave. "This is a letter from Woong's school. I forgot to send it with him today. It's already signed. It needs to go back with his things tomorrow. They just want to make sure we're all going to be careful about not sending our kids to school sick. You know how it is with that virus scare." She turned to her husband. "What's it called again? Napa? Something like that?"

"Napa's wine country." Carl opened the door to the garage. "You're talking about Nipah. The Nipah virus."

"No, you're thinking about where the Dalai Lama lives, aren't you?"

"Not Nepal, woman! Nipah. It's the Nipah virus." Beads of sweat coalesced on Carl's forehead.

"Oh, that's right. Well, that's why the school needs the letter, hon. Be sure Woong takes that form to school tomorrow or they might send him home."

Carl shook his head. "Government overreach," he mumbled.

"It's an epidemic, darling. People have been dying." Sandy's voice was patient, her southern drawl even more pronounced than normal.

"People die all the time," Carl inserted. "The way I see

12

it, when it's my time to go, nothing here's gonna dare hold me back, and that's true whether it's old age or a freak accident or Nipah virus that shoots me off to glory. Now, I'm all for basic precautions. What I'm not for is fear and paranoia. The way the media's slanting this, I guarantee you there'll be riots before the week's out. And then they'll start rounding up carriers, enforcing quarantines, it'll be 1984. It begins when the government steps in and denies parents their basic rights. Just like that little boy whose family refused chemo, remember him? Courts get a whiff of it and ..."

"I don't think Kennedy needs to worry about chemotherapy today. She just needs to remember to get Woong's form to school." She turned to Carl with a smile. "Ok, babe. You ready?"

Carl sighed, dejected. "All right. I'm off my soap box." He looked back once at Kennedy. "You be sure to call if you have any problems, you hear? Especially if your problems start in the hour to half-hour before the curtains rise at the opera. Got that?" He winked.

"Oh, you silly thing." Sandy swatted him playfully and followed him into the garage, where the St. Margaret youth group's tie-dyed Volkswagon bus waited for them. Kennedy had to chuckle at the thought of the Lindgrens actually driving that thing to dinner at Isabella's and then the opera. Since she'd never learned how to handle a stick shift, she lucked out and would keep the much more respectable Honda to take Woong to and from school.

"Have fun," she called out after them. "And happy anniversary."

CHAPTER 3

"Hey, there. How was your day?" Kennedy asked as Woong flung his backpack onto the seat next to her. Kennedy wasn't sure which surprised her more, how quickly he had learned English or how fast he'd put on weight. Last summer when the Lindgrens brought all forty-two pounds of him home from South Korea, the pediatrician had said she'd guess he was only five or six, except the orphanage workers had pieced together enough of his personal history to know he had to be at least ten, probably even a little older.

Woong sulked, and Kennedy had to remind him three times to buckle his seatbelt before they could start driving. She had no idea what an ordeal it was to pick up a child from Medford Academy. The line of cars stretched two blocks down the road. If Kennedy had been even a minute later, she would have had to wait all the way across the street or else the tail of the Honda would stick out into the intersection.

"How did school go?" Kennedy asked when she finally found an opening where she could pull out into the congested traffic.

"Ok."

"Anything interesting happen?" she pressed, remembering how much she hated these interrogation sessions with her own mother when she was Woong's age.

"We got a sub."

"Oh, yeah?"

"Uh-huh." He opened the glove compartment and pulled out one of the granola bars his mom kept perpetually stashed there. Kennedy thought about having him use some Germ-X first, but he was halfway through with his first bite, and she had to pay attention to the road. Who would have thought carpool moms could be so aggressive?

"Where was your teacher?" she asked after turning onto a side street and finally escaping the minivan gridlock.

"Went home sick."

"Oh." Kennedy glanced at Woong, who was busy peeling his second granola bar. "Hey, why don't you grab the little bottle of lotion from my backpack, ok? It's in the front zipper. Right there. Just squirt a little on your hands and rub together. It helps."

"Helps what?"

"Helps you not get sick."

"Why?"

"It kills all the germs."

"Yeah? How's it do that?"

"It breaks down the fat layer surrounding the cell walls."

"Huh?"

"Never mind. Just clean your hands before you eat any more."

After a few minutes of silence while he finished chewing, Woong asked, "Are my parents gone already?" He reached into a compartment beneath the car stereo and pulled out a baggie of goldfish crackers.

"Yeah, they left a little bit after lunch time."

"When are they getting back?"

"Tomorrow night, but you'll probably be asleep by the time they come home."

"Does that mean I get to stay up late?"

"No, you still have school the next morning."

He sighed dramatically. "I don't like school."

"Really? Why not?"

He shrugged. "Not enough snacks." He shoved some crackers into his mouth and asked, "Hey, aren't you supposed to be in school, too? Don't you go to Hogwarts or something like that?"

She smiled. "No, not Hogwarts. It's called Harvard."

"Oh. Then what's Hogwarts?"

"Something else."

"Ok. So why aren't you there now?"

"It's my spring break. We get a whole week off."

Woong kicked the heel of his sneaker against the metal bar by his feet. "Medford Academy doesn't get spring break until next week. My dad's gonna take me to a Red Sox game next Monday. That's a week from today, right?"

"Right. You know how many days that is?"

She could smell the cheddar cheese flavoring on his breath when he opened up his stuffed mouth. "Eight."

"Close. It's seven."

"No, eight."

"Seven," she repeated and rattled off the days of the week. "See? That's seven."

He shook his head. "No, 'cause today's Monday, and the game is Monday." He held up his hands to count on his fingers. "It goes Monday, Tuesday, Thursday, Wednesday, Friday, Saturday, Sunday, then another Monday. That's eight." He shoved another handful of goldfish crackers into his mouth, and Kennedy wondered if Sandy had to vacuum out the car every single day to keep it free of crumbs.

"I guess you're right." Kennedy turned on Sandy's praise

and worship CD before the discussion could digress any further. What had she gotten herself into? When Sandy first asked her to stay with Woong for the night, Kennedy hadn't thought that much about it. She didn't have any major plans for spring break. Her roommate Willow would be out with her theater friends running around New York City. If Kennedy weren't at the Lindgrens', she'd probably just be relaxing in the Harvard library. It'd been such a busy semester, she hadn't picked up a book for pleasure since Martin Luther King Day. Her entire reading list that semester was for the film as literature class she was taking. When she signed up for the course, she was expecting some Toni Morrison books, maybe a few foreign pieces, the sorts of flicks her dad didn't like ("too artsy-fartsy") and her mom didn't care for ("too many subtitles"). She didn't realize her professor was something of a Michael Crichton fanboy who apparently considered the time period between the release of *Top Gun* and the advent of *The Matrix* to be the golden age of cinematography. Oh, well. It was an easy A and a chance to get back into reading some thrillers, a genre she'd avoided when her PTSD was at its worst. The reading list, albeit unoriginal, was so extensive she found herself wishing she had time for the classics she'd grown to love. Now that the next day and a half stretched out before her, she thought of how relaxing it would be to spend the whole day reading and wondered if she was really the type who was cut out to babysit. At least Woong would be at school tomorrow. But what would they do with the rest of the day?

One hour at a time, she reminded herself.

Or maybe more like one minute.

Kennedy liked the melody of Sandy's worship song, the haunting tune, but she wasn't so sure about the lyrics. *Healed by the grace of my precious Savior.* What did that healing mean, exactly? She was still trying to figure it out. Dominic, chaplain for the Boston Police Department, said God could deliver her from her PTSD, that through the power of the Holy Spirit she could be completely free. It sounded nice. No, it sounded glorious. To be released from those talons of fear that would grip her heart at any hour of the day or night. To walk around campus without being afraid, to no longer find herself enslaved to panic, paralyzed and shaking from fear. Most of the time, she couldn't even recall what spooked her out in the first place.

As encouraging as her boyfriend tried to be, she couldn't shake the feeling this was all her fault. That if she were more spiritual, she could overcome these demons, whether they were real or figurative. Dominic had never said so, but his steadfast, unwavering faith made her feel ashamed that she still hadn't found her perfect healing. Then there were people like Sandy, people who assured her that God could heal her completely if he wanted to, but if he chose to let her PTSD remain, it was so that through her weakness, the cross of Christ would be lifted up for all to see. Kennedy was all for God getting the glory, but wouldn't he receive that much more glory and praise if he just snapped his fingers and took her trauma away?

Healed by the blood of the Lamb of God.

Woong reached out his small finger, grubby even after his liberal application of sanitizer, and punched off the music. "What're we gonna do today?"

Kennedy took a deep breath. Back on campus, she was used to waking up at six in the morning to get an early start on her fetal pig dissection before meeting her organic chemistry study group in the student union for breakfast. She could sit in a lecture hall for four hours and take practice test after practice test to prepare for the MCATs and still keep up with her Bible study and almost daily quiet time. She'd survived a kidnapping, a car chase, a skyjacking. She could handle two days with Carl and Sandy's son, couldn't she?

"Well, what do you usually do when you get home from school?"

Sandy had taken two and half hours that morning going

over Woong's schedule, but Kennedy had her suspicions that he might try to cheat the system. What kid his age wouldn't? She expected he might try to convince her his mom let him play Wii until dinner or something like that, but he shrugged and grabbed another handful of goldfish. "We go home and have snack."

"Really?"

Sandy had warned her about Woong's appetite. Now Kennedy wondered if she'd been too flippant when she told her dad there was a whole month's worth of food stashed in the Lindgrens' home. The way Woong ate, they'd be lucky to make it last until tomorrow night.

She replayed her conversation with her overly harried father. She hated the way he always tried to make her even more afraid. As if her PTSD didn't give her enough anxiety already. Kennedy wasn't worried about this Nipah virus strain. Sure, some people were dying, but that was mostly in Bangladesh where the epidemic originated and other regions in Asia. It was different here in the States, with the decent sanitation systems and top-of-the-line healthcare system. Her dad was simply caught up in the media frenzy. This would be exactly like other epidemics in the past. People got sick, and then the researchers found a vaccine. That was their job.

All that made the Nipah virus so scary was there was no known cure. Not yet. But everyone was working. A few more weeks of doctors and nurses taking extra precautions, then they'd find some way to control it, and life would go on.

Just like it always did.

"Tell me about your sub today." The praise and worship song was still stuck in Kennedy's head even though the CD was off.

Healed by the grace of my precious Savior.

"Oh, she was weird. Made us all line up at the sink and wash our hands to the happy birthday song. Twice. And she had a funny mast."

"A mast? What's that?"

"You know. Like what the man in black wears in *Princess Bride.*" He cupped his hand over his mouth and nose. "Except he wore it so people would think he was one of the bad guys, but at school she did it so she wouldn't sneeze on folks."

"I think you mean a *mask.*"

"That's what I said. It was a funny mast too. Made her look like an alligator."

Kennedy tried to guess what Woong was talking about. "An alligator? What do you mean?" The only green masks she could think of were all the way back from the World War II era. Surely a substitute wouldn't wear a gas mask in a class full of third-graders. Anyone that paranoid about catching a virus would just stay home.

Woong rolled his eyes and sighed dramatically. He clapped his hands together like Kennedy had as a little kid in Sandy's Sunday school class doing the hand motions to *Deep and Wide.* "You know. Alligator. Big teeth. Chomp chomp. I think they're in Egypt."

"That's a crocodile."

"No, crocodiles are the ones you make those funny sandal things out of. I'm talking about the big ones that eat you up in swamps."

"And your teacher's mask looked like one of those?"

"She wasn't my teacher. She was the sub."

"Right. Sorry. That's the kind of mask she had?" Kennedy wracked her brain, trying to figure out what on earth Woong was talking about.

"No, it was just colored to look like an alligator."

"Colored? Like it was green or something?"

Alligator-green sanitation masks. Maybe the Nipah outbreak would start a whole new fashion trend. She should let her roommate Willow know.

"No, it was *drawled on.*"

"The right word is *drawed*. I mean, actually it's *drawn*. It had something colored on it? Like with crayons or something?"

Woong's sigh was forceful enough to fill the entire front seats with the aroma of goldfish cracker crumbs. "No. She used a *marker*."

"I get it now." A substitute teacher who drew an animal face on a sanitation mask made a lot more sense than one who showed up in hazmat gear.

"She said she was wearing it because people are getting sick. They aren't being careful enough when they sneeze. Are you careful when you sneeze?"

Kennedy tried to maintain a serious expression. "Usually."

"Good. Because people are dying, you know."

She shot him a quick glance. "Oh, yeah? Where did you hear that?"

"Chuckie Mansfield told me at recess. His dad's a doctor, and Chuckie said they're working extra hard at his hospital getting rooms ready for all the sick people who are coming."

"Hospitals take care of sick people all the time. That's what they do." Kennedy tried to fight the nervous fluttering in her gut. Blame it on a conversation with her dad to make her anxious for the rest of the day.

"Yeah, but this sickness is really bad. Chuckie's dad says so."

Kennedy cleared her throat. "Well, then, let's pray we all stay healthy and safe."

"Ok. That's a good idea. 'Cause you're good at that kind of stuff."

"What kind of stuff?"

"You know, the praying sort of stuff. Hey, speaking of prayer, my leg's been hurting. My mom says it's growing pains, but what I'm wondering is if I ask God that he could make me grow taller without the hurting part. And maybe if I believe him hard enough I won't have no pains no more."

"Prayer doesn't work like that exactly."

"Well, my dad says we should pray for folks who are sick because sometimes God will make them well again. I was sick for a while back in Korea, you know. But then I got better. Think it's 'cause someone was praying for me then?"

"I don't know. Maybe." Kennedy wasn't used to Medford driving, or driving at all for that matter. That bank across the street didn't look familiar. Had she missed her turn?

"Yeah, I think maybe, too," Woong went on. "'Cause it was this homeless man, we called him Crazy Wu, who come and took care of me at first, and you know what? He believed in God even though he was insane."

"Oh, really?" Where was Sycamore Street? The Lindgrens lived five minutes away from Woong's school. How could she have gotten lost?

"Yeah, and he prayed for me when he found me with the sickness, and I'm guessing that's how come I got better. But that makes me think, what happens to them kids who don't have folks to pray for them, I wonder? Are they the ones who end up dying?"

"I'm sure God protects them no matter what," she mumbled. There was Sycamore. She turned abruptly, thankful there were no cops behind her to ticket her for forgetting to use her blinker. She flicked it on for a few seconds post-turn to assuage her guilt.

"Oh, I guess that make sense. I wondered about that. You know what my dad says? He says God answers all our prayers, it's just sometimes he won't do it 'til heaven. But that makes me think, what happens if two people're both praying different things, I wonder? Like what if I prayed for my mom to give me more Wii time, but she's sure it's gonna rot my brain or stuff and nonsense like that, so she gets to praying that she don't? And then even if I get to heaven where my dad says we all get our prayers answered (and he's

27

a pastor so he knows all that sorta stuff), it makes me think, what happens to my Wii in heaven? Like, will God let me play it except he won't let my mom know I'm doing it? Because that sounds sorta sneaky-like, know what I mean?"

Kennedy's brain cells were spinning as fast as the F5 cyclone in *Twister*. "That's a good question." She wondered what Dominic would say. He was always the one with the theological answers. She almost wished he weren't so strict about seeing her without anyone else around, as if they were two junior highers who needed a constant chaperone. It might be nice to put Woong to bed, throw on a movie, cuddle together on the couch. It would be two long days without anybody besides Woong to talk with. Maybe she'd try calling Willow tonight once he was asleep.

Willow had accepted Christ earlier in the semester, had prayed and asked God to forgive her sins. Kennedy wasn't so sure how much of a spiritual impact her conversion had made, though. Throughout February, the two girls had studied the Bible together. Sandy had found them a beginner's course for brand-new believers that Willow was excited to start. But then life got busy, her theater friends wanted to know why they weren't seeing her around so much, and Willow started missing their Bible study dates. After a few weeks, Kennedy got sick of asking.

And now Willow was off to New York City to binge on Broadway shows with her friends. Sandy told Kennedy to be patient with her roommate, reminded her that people grow in their faith in different ways and at different speeds. Dominic was a little more concerned that Willow's conversion hadn't resulted in the sort of fruit he said even a baby believer should exhibit. Yet another reason Kennedy felt like she had let him down.

Well, Kennedy was doing what she could. She still asked Willow every so often to come to the church meetings at Dominic's cousin's, still offered to pick up that Bible study they'd started. The irony was that the two girls were more distant from each other after Willow's prayer of salvation than they'd been when she was a die-hard atheist with a hint of agnostic leanings.

"Hey, I've got a question for you."

"Yeah? What's that?" Kennedy wasn't sure how many more questions she could take in a single car ride. She sighed with relief when the Lindgrens' cul de sac came into view.

"I've been wondering, how come God makes some people with them really springy curls in their hair? Like, there's this one girl in my class named Becky Linklater, and she's got the springiest curls you ever saw on a girl. Or a boy too, for that matter, but I'm guessing you coulda figured that out already. 'Cause I'd never seen hair like that before I come here, but my mom said that's just because God doesn't give girls in Korea hair like that. But what I want to know is, how come he doesn't? And you're not Korean, but your hair doesn't do that springy thing. At least I don't think it does, but I don't know for sure 'cause you've always got it tied up like that in your horse's tail. But do you think if you prayed God would give you curls?"

"I don't know." Kennedy let out her breath as she pulled the Honda into the Lindgrens' driveway. "Let's go in and get a snack."

Woong sprang out of the car a second before Kennedy shifted into park. "Dibs on the blue Gogurts!" he shouted.

Kennedy waited for a minute, trying to catch her mental second wind, before she yelled out after him as loudly as she could, "Hey! Wash your hands before you touch the food!"

CHAPTER 4

"How come we've got so many skin colors do you think?" Woong asked as Kennedy prepared him a third helping of ants on a log.

"What do you mean?"

"Well, like my dad, he's got that brownish skin color, but my mom, she's nearly as pale as you are except not quite so much because she's always complaining about how hot it is and how her face is always red because she's sweaty all the time."

Kennedy tried to hide her smile behind the oversized jar of peanut butter. She glanced at the label and guessed Woong had downed at least seven hundred calories in a single sitting. She knew there were chores and homework assignments to take care of, but she had a feeling Woong was preparing to move right from snack time to dinner.

God bless Sandy and her made-ahead casseroles.

Woong was still going on about different people he knew and all their skin tones. Kennedy figured for someone from a homogenous region like the Korean peninsula, seeing people of all difference races would be noteworthy.

"And that Becky Linklater, the one with all them curls I was telling you about, she's got peachy skin but brown freckles." He rolled up his sleeve and stared at his forearm. "I don't know what color you'd call me. Chuckie Mansfield says my skin's yellow, but that's not right." He picked up a banana from the fruit basket and held it against his arm. "See?"

"No. That's not yellow."

"Then what would you call it?"

"Some people say it's olive."

He frowned. "No, olives are black. I know 'cause my mom used to buy me olives, but I went through too many at once, even when she told me just two cans a day, but she caught me sneaking them. So she says I can't have olives again until summer, but I remember they were black. And I don't mean black like my dad, 'cause he's more like brown even though folks always say that's black when it's on your skin, but I mean black like my hair." He tugged on a handful to show her.

Kennedy was distracted looking for another box of raisins and only replied with a simple, "Oh."

"So what I'm wanting to know is why they'd say I'm olive colored, I wonder."

"There are other kinds of olives too. Fancy kinds that are more like …" She tilted her head to the side to study Woong. "Actually, those are usually green."

He pouted so far he could have fit at least half a dozen raisins on his lower lip. "I'm not green. But I seen folks who were green before. Back before I came here, you know how I was a flower swallow and taking care of myself on the streets? Well, some of them other flower swallows got so sick they turned green. I don't mean green like broccoli, more green like that pea soup my mom makes. Have you ever had pea soup? I think it's funny because peas are green like broccoli-green, but when you turn them into soup it's a different kind of green, like green and brown all mixed together, and what I'm wanting to know is why that is, I wonder."

"I have no idea." Kennedy set another plate in front of him with ten new celery sticks smothered in peanut butter and raisins.

"I wonder why they call these ants. 'Cause I've ate ants before, did you know that? Back during the hunger I did. And they weren't too bad, neither. But I'm glad I don't have to eat them now on account of folks here thinking it's gross. But you're a scientist, right? So you're used to things like that, so I'm guessing you don't think it's too gross, do you?"

"I suppose not if you're hungry enough."

"I liked ants, but grasshoppers were better. 'Course, that might have been on account of them being bigger, so you get fuller faster. You ever tried grasshopper?"

"No. I haven't."

He shrugged and took a noisy bite out of one of his celery sticks. "You'd like them if you tried them, I'm guessing, except they make a bad crunch, and sometimes girls don't like that part of it. But you're different, right? I mean, not really a girly kind of girl, aren't you?"

"That depends on what you mean."

Kennedy's phone beeped. Thankful for a distraction, she hopped to her feet and picked it up off the counter.

A text message from her dad.

Thirteen new confirmed cases in New York today.

It was three in the morning in Yanji. She couldn't guess if her dad was staying up late or getting up early. Either way, she knew he kept his eyes glued to his computer screen, his mouse continually ready to refresh his news page.

If a baby elephant in an Australian zoo came down with the Nipah virus, Kennedy would hear about it.

Another beep.

Nine deaths in Florida.

Well, it was a good thing she wasn't in Florida or New

York, then. She washed her hands again since she was already so near the sink and then sat down by Woong. "Do you have much homework tonight?"

He shook his head. "Nah. Just a spelling test to practice. My mom says you're supposed to help me study. But what I'm wanting to know is how come we need to spell the words as long as we know how to say them, I wonder. 'Cause if you can say the word just fine, everyone knows what you're talking about."

"Sometimes we do things because our parents or teachers tell us to." It was the only answer Kennedy had the energy to offer.

Woong sighed dramatically. "Yeah. I can't wait to be big like you. 'Cause then nobody would ever tell me what to do. Like I could stay up all night long if I wanted and play video games like Mr. Nick from my dad's church does. Or watch as many movies as I wanted, even if they've got too much sword fighting in them. Or I could go weeks without cleaning my room at all. I'm pretty sure Mr. Nick does that too, by the way, 'cause I've been in his house before, and it's so messy you can't hardly even find a place to sit. That's what I can do when I'm all grown up. And if I got a little sick, my mom wouldn't go around worrying and telling me I hafta take some yucky medicine or eat up all my chicken soup when it hardly counts as soup because it's nearly all water."

Kennedy was about to explain how it's sometimes nice to be taken care of like that when you're not feeling well, but her phone beeped again.

A third text from her dad.

First confirmed fatality in Boston. Don't go anywhere that isn't absolutely necessary.

CHAPTER 5

"Hey, you know what I'm wanting to know? It's how come we've got to sleep at all, I wonder. Cause Chuckie Mansfield says he's got a pet goldfish, and goldfish never sleep. But what I wonder is how you'd know if your goldfish really was asleep or not, know what I mean? But his dad's a doctor so he knows that sorta stuff, and that's what he says. So if goldfish don't hafta sleep, how come you and me got to? And why do kids always hafta do it earlier than grown-ups? It's an abomination." He scrunched up his face in a perfect imitation of his father behind his pulpit.

Kennedy, guessing the impression wasn't intentional, masked her laugh with a cough.

"You better be careful," Woong said. "When you cough on somebody, that gives them your germs."

"You're right." She pulled Woong's Iron Man sheets up to his chin. "Now, your mom says you like to read before bed, so should we start that now?"

"Well first, what I'm wanting to know is how come people have adversaries to start with."

"Why they have what?"

"Adversaries."

"Like enemies?"

"No, I mean like what my mom and dad are doing."

Kennedy remained clueless.

"You know," Woong exclaimed, clearly exasperated. "*Adversaries.* When you go away and leave your kids with strangers."

Kennedy didn't know if she should chuckle or feel sorry for him. "Well, first of all, I'm not a stranger. I come over here all the time."

"Yeah, but …"

"And second of all," she interrupted, "even when your parents go away for a night, they love you just as much as when they're here. That's why your mom's going to make a special point to call you tonight even when she and your dad are at the theater. And why she made so much good food for us to eat. Like that lasagna we had for dinner. Wasn't that yummy?"

"Yeah. Are there any leftovers? Sometimes Mom heats me up leftovers for breakfast once I finish my box of cereal."

"We'll check and see in the morning, ok?" Kennedy still

hadn't cleaned up the kitchen. She'd been too busy quizzing Woong on his spelling words. She had no idea how an inquisitive child like him could stretch out a study session to the rate of one word per half an hour. When your teacher's given you a list of fifteen spelling words ...

"So what are you and your parents reading at night?"

"It's my mom who reads. Dad's too busy playing the Wii."

"Oh, yeah?" She tried to hide a grin at the idea of Carl engrossed in video games.

"Yeah, he likes to do that golf one. Mom says it's because he works so hard during the rest of the day he's allowed to do it at night. But she never sets the timer for him." He pouted.

"Well, sometimes adults get special privileges."

"Yeah, like Mrs. Winifred."

"Who?"

"My teacher. She got to leave early from school today because she was sick. My mom never lets me stay home from school, even when I have a sore throat. But all Mrs. Winifred had to do was tell the principal she had a fever, and she got to go home for the rest of the day. That's how come we got a substituent."

"You mean substitute?"

"Yeah. That's what I said."

"All right." Kennedy tried to remember what she and Woong were supposed to do next. He'd brushed his teeth after asking about two dozen questions about cavities, dentists, and braces. ("'Cause Chuckie Mansfield, his teeth are so crooked he says he's gonna need them metal things on them once he gets a little bigger, except he still has to wait for some of his first set of teeth to fall out first before it's ready, and that got me to thinking how come we got two different sorts of teeth to start with and why God didn't just make us with the ones we could use always.")

She glanced at the clock. Woong was already thirty minutes past his usual lights out time. Carl and Sandy would call as soon as intermission started at the opera, which could be any minute. She sighed. "Ok, are you ready to read?"

"Yup," he answered, snuggling down beneath his sheets. "I've been wondering what's going to happen to Violet now that she's sick, 'cause I know kids can take care of themselves even if they don't have a boxcar to live in. That's how I done it before I got adopted, you know, but it gets a lot harder if you have the sickness on account of you not being able to do anything for yourself, even get yourself someplace clear to barf. Have you read *The Boxcar*

Children? Do you think Violet's gonna be ok, or do you think she might die on account of the sickness?"

"She'll be just fine." Kennedy figured a vague spoiler was justified when she saw how scared Woong looked.

He let out his breath. "Well, I've been wondering, you know, even though of course she's just a girl in a book and not a real kid at all, and I've never read a book where a kid actually dies, but I suppose it's possible, don't you think? And then I figure it's not really a book I'd wanna read, 'cause don't most people read so they can think about happy things, not things that really do happen like kids dying?"

Kennedy wondered how much Woong had endured as a street child before he found himself in the South Korean orphanage. Even Carl and Sandy were still piecing together the details of his hard life before he joined their family.

Kennedy opened up *The Boxcar Children* to where a piece of large, floral-patterned stationary marked off a new chapter. She read the first few sentences. "Does this sound right?" she asked. "Is this where your mom left off last?"

"Uh-huh. I think so."

She let her mind turn onto autopilot as she began to read.

"Why's it so cold in here?" Woong asked half a paragraph in.

Kennedy hadn't noticed anything wrong with the temperature. She pulled a blanket up over Woong. "Here you go." She started to read again.

"You know what I'm thinking?" he interrupted a few minutes later.

"What?"

"How come they thought their grandfather was so mean? 'Cause they didn't ever really know him, and I've never had a grandfather, least not one that I really remember, but in all the other stories the grandfathers are always nice. Like in the sword-fighting movie my mom doesn't like, there's a really nice grandpa in that one. He comes and reads to the little boy when he's sick even though at first the boy thinks it's just a kissing book or stuff and nonsense like that. Or there's that dancing story at Christmastime where the girl gets that funny toy doll thingy, right? And I think it's her grandfather who gives it to her but I'm not really sure, 'cause, you know, there's no talking in that one, so unless you already know what it's about, it's kinda hard to guess what's going on, know what I mean?"

Kennedy decided she'd make it through the first page and call it a night. How did Sandy handle these incessant questions all day long? Woong was a sweet kid, really bright. But Kennedy felt like she needed a twelve-hour nap just to recover from his chatter. She finally reached the third paragraph after just as many interruptions when the Lindgrens' home phone rang. She handed Woong the book. "Save our spot. I'll go see who that is." She had expected Carl and Sandy to call her on her cell to say good-night to Woong, but maybe they were calling the house instead.

"Lindgrens' residence," she answered.

"Hi, is this Woong's mother?"

Kennedy didn't recognize the worried voice on the other line.

"No, this is ..." She hesitated. Two years and thousands of miles away from home, and she still couldn't get over her dad's paranoia about admitting when she was in a house by herself. "This is Kennedy, a friend of the family."

"I see. Is Mrs. Lindgren there?"

"I'm afraid she's unavailable right now. Can I take a message?"

"Maybe. This is Margot Linklater. My daughter Becky goes to school with Woong?"

"Oh, right." Kennedy hoped Woong hadn't gotten into trouble in the classroom.

"I'm calling to get more details of what happened in school today?" She ended nearly all her sentences as a question.

Uh-oh. Was Kennedy about to have to step in as referee between a third-grader and an angry mother? "I'm not sure what you mean."

"Their teacher. Mrs. Winifred. My Becky tells me she nearly fainted in class."

Kennedy paused. "Woong said something to me about her leaving early, but I don't think he mentioned fainting."

Mrs. Linklater's voice lowered. "I'm just wondering if the school is giving us all the details."

"What do you mean?"

"Well, my Becky was very concerned. She said Mrs. Winifred was so sick she couldn't stand up. And it came on so suddenly. And according to another family, Mrs. Winifred had a fever …" She left the thought unfinished.

"Are you worried about Nipah virus?" Kennedy asked, hoping she didn't sound too incredulous.

"Aren't we all?"

Apparently so.

"I'm sure we would have heard if it was something that serious." Kennedy strained her ears, trying to hear if Woong was making any noise from the other end of the hall.

"That's what I'm saying," Mrs. Linklater went on. "Worst-case scenario, if their teacher was that sick and got herself to the hospital today, it's still at least a full day or two before they'd get back any reports from the CDC, and then who knows how many kids may have been exposed, or heaven forbid actually infected?"

Kennedy wanted to say there was nothing at all to worry about, but what did she know? She lived most of her life with her head buried in her studies. If it hadn't been for her dad's constant text updates, she'd have no idea how far the Nipah virus had spread already or how many people were as worried as Mrs. Linklater.

"I don't want to overstep my place," she said, "but you might want to let Mrs. Lindgren know that several of us are going to be pulling our kids out for the next few days until we get some clearer answers of what's going on. You know, they've closed several schools in New York already."

No, she didn't know that. She was surprised her dad hadn't texted to tell her.

"Ok, I'll pass that on." She took a breath, thankful that it wasn't too choppy. A major panic attack while she was home alone with Woong was the last thing anybody needed.

"Tell Mrs. Lindgren she's welcome to call me if she has any questions, all right? She's got my number."

"Ok, thank you so much. I'll pass that on."

"I'm sorry to bother you so late. I'm sure Woong is dead to the world by now. I hope the phone ringing didn't wake him."

"No, don't worry about that." Kennedy had no idea how many other students at Medford Academy were *dead to the world* by 9:15, but Woong Lindgren certainly wasn't one of them. She thanked Mrs. Linklater for the call and hung up.

"Was that my parents?" Woong asked when Kennedy returned to his room. He was sitting up in bed, flipping ahead in *The Boxcar Children*.

"No, but they'll call as soon as intermission starts."

"What's intermission?"

"The part in the middle of the show they're at where they all take a break."

"You mean like halftime?"

"Yeah, like halftime. Want to keep reading until they call?"

He pouted in thought. "Ok. But you're sure Violet's gonna be ok?"

"I'm sure. I read that book like ten times or more when I was your age. She'll be just fine."

He let out his breath. "Good. 'Cause I seen people with the sickness, and trust me, it's not something you read about right before you go to bed. 'Least not if you don't want nightmares."

CHAPTER 6

Kennedy woke up the next morning to the sound of her cell screeching. As soon as she remembered what she was doing in the Lindgrens' guest room, she reached to turn off her alarm only to realize it was her dad calling.

"Hello?" She hated the way her voice sounded so groggy in the morning. Oh, well. What did he expect when he woke her up at such ungodly hours of the day and night? How early was it, anyway?

"What's the name of the school Carl and Sandy's son goes to?" her dad snapped. "Is it a charter school?"

Kennedy blinked at the digital clock beside her on the night table. 8:20? Had she forgotten to set her alarm? She was supposed to wake up Woong an hour ago.

"I'm running late, Dad. Can I call you back?"

"What's the name of his school?" he repeated.

She dragged herself up to a sitting position, wondering what it would be like to have a normal father who lived in a normal American town and who engaged in normal hobbies

47

instead of being a perpetual news junkie.

"He goes to Medford Academy, and we both slept in." At least, she hoped Woong had slept in instead of waking up early and getting into trouble. After today, Sandy wouldn't even trust Kennedy to look after a pet parakeet. "I've got to get him up or he's going to be late."

"No, he's not. Neither of you are going anywhere."

Kennedy wasn't ready for her dad's dramatics. A five-minute shower, that's what she needed. No, there wasn't time for that. A two-minute shower then. Anything to clear away this mental fog.

"Medford Academy's closed," her dad said. "Something about one of the teachers possibly coming down with Nipah. What grade's Carl and Sandy's little boy in? First?" Her dad always assumed children were younger than they really were, which probably explained why he worried about Kennedy as if she were a preteen about to go away to her first ever sleep-away camp.

Kennedy put her phone on speaker while she checked out the Channel 2 News website. Her dad was right. Sheila Winifred, a 57-year-old veteran teacher at Medford Academy, admitted herself into the hospital yesterday morning with fever, disorientation, and swelling of the brain. The article was carefully phrased, with words like *suspicion* and *possibility* heavily sprinkled throughout. Even though Mrs. Winifred's case couldn't be confirmed yet as Nipah, enough symptoms matched and enough parents were worried that the superintendent closed down Medford Academy until the CDC reports came back. Other schools in the district would remain open, although parents were urged to keep children home if they showed any signs of illness.

Kennedy stared at the webpage and thought back to her brief conversation last night with that nervous mom from Woong's school. Had Kennedy's dad's irrational fears infected everyone around her? Or was this more than paranoia? Schools didn't just close their doors without good reason. Was it really possible that …

"All right, Kensie girl, what's your plan?" Her dad asked the question as if he didn't already have an answer ready to dictate to her.

"I guess we stay home, and I'll try to figure out what to do to keep Woong entertained all day." Maybe she'd call Sandy and ask her to bend the rules a little bit so he could have extra Wii time.

"Not good enough." Her dad had an unassuming voice, but he could bark orders when it came to Kennedy's personal safety. "You've got to assume that Carl and Sandy's boy — what's his name again?"

"Woong. His name is Woong."

"Right. You've got to assume that Woong's been exposed. What makes Nipah so scary and dangerous is the incubation period. You can be a carrier for a couple days before coming down with any signs of illness. We have to be conservative and give it a full week to see if you're symptomatic. You know what to look for, right? And you've got to act quick, because they're talking about people going from feeling perfectly fine to ending up at the ER in the course of an hour, just like that teacher. It starts with fever, flu-like symptoms, headaches ..."

Kennedy was startled by noise at the doorway, and she snatched up her phone. Punching off the speaker, she interrupted her father's WebMD recitation.

"Dad, I really got to go. I can call back real soon, I promise."

"But wait a minute, we still haven't figured out ..."

Kennedy turned off the phone and stared at the tiny boy in his Hulk slippers standing in the doorway. His wide eyes didn't change when she beckoned him into the room.

"You ok, little buddy?" she asked, certain he wasn't.

"Was that your dad?"

"Yeah." She forced a smile. "He worries a lot about germs and stuff. He's kind of funny that way." She mentally rehearsed the last few minutes of their conversation. How much had Woong overheard?

"It's the sickness, isn't it? Teacher has the sickness."

Kennedy sighed. Why had she been so stupid as to put the phone on speaker? And why couldn't her dad tone down his end-of-the-world dramatics for a change?

Kennedy had made herself a promise that when she became a doctor she would always be honest with patients, although now she understood how toning down the truth could become a tempting option. "It's probably not Nipah, but they're going to close the school for a few days just to be sure."

She hoped the mention of an impromptu holiday might be enough to shatter Woong's fearful demeanor.

No such luck. "Is she gonna die?"

"No, little guy." Well, technically she wasn't qualified to make that promise, so she added a hasty, "At least, none of us really think so. Your principal's just doing what he needs to do to keep everyone safe so other people don't get sick."

"You mean *I* might get sick?"

Kennedy kicked herself. It was becoming more and more clear that she'd never be fit for a job in pediatrics.

"You just keep washing your hands and eating healthy foods, and you'll probably be fine." She forced a smile and wished Sandy were here. Of all the times for her and Carl to leave on an anniversary getaway ... "Come on." She went to take Woong's hand before figuring he was probably too old for that. She walked down the hall and turned around. "You coming?"

He frowned. "My legs hurt again."

She gave him a sympathetic smile. "We've got some extra time. Why don't you help me make a big breakfast to start off our day, ok? Keep your mind off your growing pains. What sounds good to you?"

"Teacher getting better." Woong stared at his massive Hulk slippers. "That's what sounds good to me."

You and me both, little buddy.

Kennedy left the thought unspoken.

CHAPTER 7

It was eleven before Kennedy cleared off the breakfast table and started a load of dishes. Woong had helped her make pancakes, except his version of *helping* involved asking about a dozen questions about each of the ingredients and why she was adding them in the way she was ("'Cause I've watched my mom make pancakes millions of times before, and she doesn't ever do it like that").

She finally got hold of Carl and Sandy just before noon. They hadn't heard the reports about Medford Academy closing but decided to head straight home. Kennedy felt bad that their anniversary getaway was cut short, but she was grateful she wouldn't have to stay here worrying about Woong by herself for much longer.

Woong was busy cleaning up his room. At least, that's what he was supposed to be doing, but Kennedy guessed by the crashing noises and numerous movie quotes coming from the bedroom that he was practicing his sword-fighting skills and pretending to be on the set of *Princess Bride*. As long as he was happy and content …

Kennedy stared at the overflowing sink. She should have never let the dishes get so far behind. It would take two loads just to catch up, and she had a nagging suspicion Woong would be coming out of his room any minute, "wanting to know what time we're gonna have some lunch." Kennedy didn't feel like spending another minute in the kitchen. There was about a serving and a half of lasagna left over from last night, but that was hardly more than an appetizer the way Woong ate. She leaned over the stack of casserole dishes in the fridge. Chicken stir fry? Chili mac and cheese? She pulled out a small round container labeled *pork and bean soup*. That would work. She stared again at the messy sink, wondering if she should start washing the bigger things by hand.

She had just rolled up her sleeves when someone knocked outside.

"I'll get it!" Woong yelled, and Kennedy couldn't intercept him before he flung open the front door.

"Hey, Mr. Nick!"

"Hey, buddy!" Nick, the youth pastor at Carl and Sandy's church, raised his hand so Woong could give him a high-five. "Fist bump!" He held out his knuckles. Kennedy tried not to think of how many germs the two of them had just exchanged.

"Guess what!" Woong shouted. "There's no school today."

Kennedy was glad to hear the chipper excitement back in his tone.

Nick grinned and squatted down until he was eye level with Woong. "That's right. You guys get a vacation, don't you?"

"Yeah."

"Well, don't waste all that time on the Wii. Growing boy like you's got better things to do." Nick shut the door behind him and turned toward Kennedy, his blond dreadlocks flinging around after him. "Hey, there. How's it going?"

She glanced at his shirt. It had a stick figure kneeling by a bedside and a caption that read, *Prayer Warriors. Because real history makers do it on their knees.*

"Fine," she answered. She hadn't even been home alone with Woong for a full twenty-four hours, and she was already grateful for the chance to talk to a human being taller than four feet.

"Sorry to barge in like this. I was going to call while I was riding over here, and then I forgot until I was like two minutes away." He nodded to the window, where Kennedy could see his bicycle leaning on the Lindgrens' front porch. "I was hoping I could borrow the Honda. There's a few things I need to pick up from the store. You both could come along too if you wanted."

"Yeah!" Woong shouted.

"Probably not," Kennedy told him. "I think your parents want you to stay here where you'll be sure not to catch any other germs."

"Yeah, kind of crazy what's going on, isn't it?" Nick fidgeted with one of his dreads.

Crazy was one way of putting it.

"I think we'll stay here, but you're welcome to take the Honda. It's in the garage with the keys hanging up on the peg."

"All right." He stepped in the entryway. "What's that smell? It's delicious."

"Just some bean soup for lunch."

"Wow, I didn't know you could cook."

"I'm only reheating it. Sandy made it."

Nick nodded. "Oh, so that explains it."

"You can stay if you'd like a bite." Kennedy knew Nick was in the habit of eating over at the Lindgrens' several nights a week. It was probably the only way he sustained himself on his bachelor diet of frozen meals and Ramen noodles.

"Nah, I've got to go. My buddy just posted a picture of

the canned food aisle at Rory's. Everyone's stocking up. It's gonna be an interesting couple of weeks."

While Nick was talking, Kennedy had been trying to lure him away from listening ears, but Woong wouldn't leave until Kennedy finally told him to go wash his hands in the bathroom. "And do the happy birthday song twice like you learned at school," she called after him.

Nick followed her into the kitchen and paused by the door that led to the garage. "I know Carl and Sandy usually have plenty on hand. You guys going to be all right if things get hard?"

He was laid back about most things. Kennedy didn't picture him as the type to get worked up over a potential outbreak. The fact that so many other people besides her father were taking this Nipah scare seriously was more worrisome than the news stories themselves.

"How hard do you expect it to get?" she asked.

He shrugged. "Most people are saying it's going to get worse before it gets better. A shame, really. I don't even want to know what this whole scare is going to do to worsen the refugee crisis."

Kennedy had hardly thought through the medical ramifications of the disease. She wasn't ready to jump straight to politics. "Are you going to be ok if they don't have any food at the store?" she asked. "Do you want to take one of these casseroles with you in case the shelves are already empty?"

"No, I'll be all right. If I get to Rory's and can't find anything, maybe I'll take you up on it, but I think if I hurry now I'll get there before they're completely sold out."

Woong was already out of the bathroom, so she was glad Nick didn't say anything else about the epidemic.

"So the keys are hanging up in their usual spot?"

"Yeah."

"All right, I'll bring the car back as soon as I'm done." He opened the door that led to the garage.

"No rush," Kennedy called after him. Where did she and Woong have to go, anyway?

After Nick left, Kennedy served up two large bowls of soup.

"Want to play a game of cards while we eat?" Woong asked.

"Sure. That sounds like a fun idea."

Woong jumped up and ran to the game closet, and Kennedy glanced at the text coming in from her dad.

Governor of New York declared a state of emergency.

Another beep.

Two deaths reported in New Hampshire. One a 10-year-old boy.

Kennedy put her phone on vibrate.

"You want to play Uno or Egyptian rat race?" Woong asked.

Kennedy had never heard of Egyptian rat race. "Let's do Uno." She couldn't remember how long it been since she'd last played it. Probably at least a decade.

Her phone shook again, and she turned it face down so she didn't have to see whatever depressing news her dad was sending her now.

"Bring the deck here," she told Woong, "and I'll deal while you start your lunch. Don't want to let your mom's soup get cold."

CHAPTER 8

Kennedy always assumed Uno was a game of pure chance, which was a statistic impossibility given how many games Woong won in a row. They had eaten up the entire pot of soup, and Woong had finished off the leftover lasagna, too. Carl and Sandy were due back in less than an hour. The house was disastrous, but at least the day with Woong had gone relatively smoothly.

"You got any other games you want to play instead?" she asked after Woong beat her for the sixth or seventh time at Uno.

"Hmm." Woong pouted. "Maybe Battleship?"

"Sure. Why not?" At the very least, it was a nice way to procrastinate from having to work on that next load of dishes.

Woong had just put the cards away, and the two of them were setting up their battle stations when someone knocked on the front door.

"Is that Mr. Nick?" Woong's eyes lit up.

"Might be," Kennedy answered, although she couldn't figure out why he'd go around to the front door after dropping the car off in the garage.

Woong followed her to the main entrance. Kennedy glanced through the window at the familiar face on the porch and threw open the door.

"Woah! Is that pink hair?" Woong shouted. "Inconceivable!"

Kennedy stepped aside to let her roommate into the Lindgrens' home. "What are you doing here?" she asked.

"Well, if you'd been getting my messages, you would have known," Willow answered. "Let me guess. You let your batteries die again?"

Kennedy rolled her eyes. "No, I just turned it on vibrate. My dad kept sending me his end-of-the-world texts." She gave her roommate a hug. "What's going on? I thought you'd be in New York by now."

"Yeah, the trip got cancelled." Willow flung her magenta-streaked hair behind her ear. "Nobody really wants to be in New York right now. It's not just your dad who's freaking out about this whole …"

"Hey, Woong," Kennedy interrupted, "can you do me a big favor and clear the dishes off the table?"

He pouted but left the two girls alone in the entryway.

"So I guess it's getting pretty bad?" she asked Willow when he was out of earshot.

"I'll say. You heard about that teacher from … Oh, shhhhh …" Willow stopped herself. "I mean, oh rats. That kid goes to that school doesn't he? The one with the teacher. That's why he's home today. Geeze, I didn't even think about that. Are you ok? Do you think either of you got exposed?"

Kennedy glanced down the hall, hoping Woong wasn't listening. "I think we're ok. I mean, the chances of infection are really low."

"Yeah." Willow ran her fingers through her hair. Kennedy wouldn't be surprised if she came up with a quick excuse to leave, and she certainly wouldn't blame her.

"Kennedy!" Woong shouted from the kitchen, drawing out each syllable. "What're we having for a snack?"

"I swear that kid eats like an elephant," she muttered.

"I have an idea!" Woong called. "Why don't you get two cups of juice, and I'll put poison in one of them and you'll have to decide which one you want to drink?"

Willow raised her penciled eyebrows.

"He just watched *The Princess Bride* for the first time," Kennedy explained.

Willow nodded. "Got it. Well, want some help with

62

figuring out a snack?" she asked. "I've got my mom's carrot-carob-zucchini drop recipe on my phone. Does your pastor keep any garbanzo bean flour on hand?"

"I don't think so." She glanced at the door. "Do you want to stay a while? I mean, you're welcome to, but if you're worried about getting sick ..."

"Pffft." Willow tossed her hair. "You know me. I'd go absolutely crazy in my dorm room all day. If I'm not hanging out here, I'd probably be at the mall exposing myself to every pathogen known to humankind. I've been taking zinc droplets since I was two weeks old. I've got a wicked strong immune system. Besides, it's not like either you or the kid are sick, right? I mean, this is all just precautions at this point, isn't it?"

"Kennedy!" Woong shrieked again.

"What?" Kennedy ignored Willow's bemused grin.

"Can you make some popcorn while we play Battleship?"

Kennedy glanced at her roommate. "So you want to hang out for a while?"

Willow shrugged. "Not like I've got anything better to do. You have no idea how bad it sucks. Oh wait, is *sucks* one of those words that's gonna get me in trouble? I know this is a pastor's house and all."

Kennedy wished Willow hadn't flaked out on their new-believer's Bible study. They could actually talk about things like grace versus legalism. She was pretty sure Willow pictured the entire Christian life as a big list of dos and don'ts. No wonder she hadn't kept up her original spiritual momentum.

"You're fine," she said. "Just be careful around Woong. I don't think his parents let him use that word."

"Ok, I'll be good. I promise." Willow shot her a dazzling smile, and the two girls walked into the dining room.

Woong was sitting in front of his Battleship display, shielding it from view. "What's for snack?" He scrunched up his eyes and stared at Willow. "And why's her hair that color? Were you born that way, or did you get it painted?"

"Dyed," Kennedy corrected.

"Who died?" Woong's eyes widened. "Someone died?"

"No, I was just talking about Willow's hair."

"Her hair's dead? Do you mean all the way dead or just mostly dead? 'Cause there's a difference, you know."

"I just mean when you color your hair, you say that it's *dyed*."

"Dead."

"What?"

"You can't say that something is *died*. You say something is *dead*. That's better grammar."

"Ok." Kennedy chose to drop the vocabulary lesson. "Hey, listen. Your mom and dad are coming home early, so you ..."

"They are?"

"Yeah, so you need to go get your room extra clean so it's perfect by the time they get back, ok?"

Woong cocked his head to the side. "What do I get if I do a good enough job?"

Kennedy wasn't in the habit of entering into negotiations with third-graders. "Popcorn?"

He frowned. "No. You need to ask me what I want."

"Fine. What do you want?"

He put on his most serious facial expression. "I want my father back, you ..."

"All right," she interrupted quickly. "That's enough movie quotes for today. Go clean up."

The excitement in his eyes clouded over, and he slumped away from the table with a half-hearted, "Ok."

Kennedy started to clear the table, wondering how long it would take her to get the kitchen presentable again.

"Looks like we're on the set of *Titanic* before everyone dies," Willow stated helpfully.

Kennedy didn't respond. She was busy glancing through the texts she'd missed from her dad. More casualties. More confirmed cases. More states. More cities. More lists of symptoms to look out for. Kennedy browsed through the list and figured anyone with a pulled hamstring, ear infection, or stubbed toe could find a way to convince themselves they were about to die.

She sighed.

Willow glanced up from the Battleship board she'd been looking over. "What's wrong?"

"Oh, just my dad."

"Yeah, I bet he's freaking out about this whole thing."

"He's been freaking out for the past three weeks." Kennedy remembered the day the first Nipah case was confirmed in the States. Her dad wanted her to go to the nearest drugstore and buy a case of at least a hundred face masks, fully expecting her to wear one every time she went out in public. He told her not to eat anything cooked in the cafeteria but to buy canned things and heat them up in her dorm room after washing her hands with antibacterial soap and ideally a few additional squirts of Germ-X.

Kennedy tuned him out at that point, told herself he was overreacting. Was this like the boy who cried wolf? Had her dad freaked her out so many times in the past over inconsequential nothings that now, when her life really might be in danger, she'd chosen to all but completely ignore his instructions?

"Don't let him get under your skin." Willow gave her a reassuring rub on the shoulder. "He's just trying to look out for you."

"Yeah, I know."

One more load of dishes later, Kennedy and Willow sat across from each other sharing some of Sandy's raspberry tea. Woong's battle sounds and impressively accurate impressions of Andre the Giant from the back room told Kennedy he was at least happy, even if he wasn't cleaning.

"I'm sorry you couldn't make it to New York," Kennedy said. That's all Willow had been talking about for weeks. "You must be really disappointed."

Willow let out a melodramatic sigh. "Yes and no. I mean, it totally blows ... I mean, it totally *stinks* that I'm gonna miss all those shows, you know? I was really looking forward to that. But then there's part of me that thinks I actually jinxed myself out of it. I don't know. Does the Bible say anything about jinxes, or is that too hocus-pocus for Christians to believe in?"

"What do you mean?"

"Well, I was gonna be hanging out with all my friends. I mean, it wasn't only about Broadway, of course. And I've been trying to cut back on certain things now that I'm saved. I'm not saying I'm doing a perfect job, and you probably know that better than anyone else, but I swear to … I mean, I can *honestly say* I'm trying really hard. But that's just the thing. You made it sound like I ask Jesus into my heart, I ask him to forgive me of my sins, and then he gives me so much joy and happiness and hope it's like I never look back on all the stuff I had to leave behind. I mean, can you believe I haven't smoked a single joint in six weeks? I'm serious. I don't think I've been this clean since before I started getting periods. I'm not joking."

Kennedy glanced down the hall just to make sure Woong hadn't popped out of his room to eavesdrop.

"And at first, it was sort of like that. That joy and stuff. A little bit." She shrugged. "I mean, I felt something at least. And then that Bible study we were doing, it kept talking about all these things like those spiritual fruits and all that stuff, and I'm sure it's great, but it just made me realize how far I've got to go to be like you. I mean, the vocabulary, everything. It was as bad as if I were to jump into your organic chemistry class mid-semester and even though you offered to be my study partner, you couldn't figure out why I couldn't keep up. I mean, I don't even know the difference between an atom and a molecule without looking it up, but you'd be talking about chemical equations and *blah blabetty blah blah* stuff like that, and that's kind of how it's felt these past couple months. Like you're so far ahead I'm bound to disappoint you. I mean, I'm already disappointed in myself."

Kennedy didn't know what to say. She wanted to apologize, but Willow kept on talking.

"When I prayed with you that night and asked Jesus into my heart or whatever you want to call it, that night I told him I wanted him to forgive my sins, I really meant it. You said if I was sincere, he'd answer my prayers. And then the first few weeks passed, and the novelty sort of died down. I don't know if that's my fault or what, but it did, and then all of a sudden I realized what a hypocrite I was, and I don't know if you can understand this, being a goody-goody God's girl and all that. And I don't say that to be mean — I seriously envy you. Because it's so easy for you. You've never slept around, you're as clean as a whistle, your boyfriend's like Mr. Chastity Belt or whatever the male equivalent of that is, and it all just comes so easy to you. But here I am, I'm trying my hardest, and I keep waiting for that joy and stuff you told me was supposed to happen when I got saved, except it didn't. At least not for very long. I kept going through the motions for a little while, doing our Bible study and all that, but I knew myself. I hadn't really changed.

"So New York came up, and I really wanted to go be with my friends. I'm sure if I had asked, you would have told me it was a bad idea. Hanging out with all those old influences. But you never said I had to stop being friends with everyone from the past when I became a Christian. And I wanted to go. I felt a little guilty about it. I knew there'd be drinking and stuff going on. I didn't really want to get back involved in that, but by then it'd been so long since I'd felt anything of that happiness you promised me that I figured I may as well go to New York with my friends and just see what happened. It wasn't like I was planning to jump off the wagon there or anything, but who would have been that surprised if I did, you know?

"So when I heard today the trip got cancelled, I got even more freaked out. Like maybe God's mad at me for thinking about going in the first place. And you never said it counts as sin before you've actually done something wrong, but maybe it does. Or maybe I'm not saved at all. Because if I was, I probably shouldn't be experiencing all these temptations and things. I'm just starting to wonder if it really worked that night I prayed. Maybe I didn't believe hard enough. I tried. I swear to ... I mean, *I promise* I tried as hard as I could. But what if it wasn't enough faith? What if it didn't count? So now, I've given up my friends, my fun, and

I don't even get heaven out of it. Excuse my language, but that just sucks."

"Yeah. You're right."

Willow leaned forward in her seat. "Huh?"

"I was just thinking out loud. And I mean, you're right. If you give up all the fun of the world and don't get anything out of it, that's a terrible exchange." She didn't know what else she was supposed to say. She'd been so excited last winter when Willow's finally accepted Christ. It was the first time Kennedy had shared the gospel with anybody, and a new soul had been accepted into the family of God. What could be more thrilling? And then the weeks passed, and Willow's enthusiasm for her new-found faith started to wane, and Kennedy was left wondering what went wrong.

She still wondered what went wrong. Had she given Willow false promises? Wasn't God's Spirit supposed to be enough to make up for the party-life she had left behind?

"I wish I knew what to tell you," she sighed. If Sandy were here, she'd have all kinds of encouragement to pour out into Willow's spirit. In fact, the very first weekend after Willow got saved, Sandy had the two girls over for a huge barbecue ribs feast with a side of tofu stir-fry for Willow. It was the same night she gave Kennedy and Willow that new-believer's Bible study to go through. It should have worked.

Willow frowned into her cup. "Well, they say religious fervor is genetically inherited. Maybe I'm just not one of the lucky ones."

There had to be another explanation. What could Kennedy say? She needed to talk to Dominic. He always had the right words of wisdom to offer in situations like these. Two years ago, Kennedy might have told Willow to pray and read her Bible more. That seemed to be the catch-all solution to anybody interested in growing in their spiritual walk. But after suffering for over a year now from her PTSD, Kennedy realized that daily devotions weren't some sort of Band-Aid you could throw on whenever you wanted a spiritual pick-me-up. There was more to it than that.

She just didn't know what.

"I'm really sorry you've been struggling like this. You should have told me sooner." She tried not to make her voice sound accusatory. Willow was suffering from enough guilt as it was.

"Yeah, well, I didn't want to bother you. I mean, like I said, you've had it so easy ..."

"Maybe that's what happened," Kennedy interrupted, still thinking out loud and hoping that somehow God might show up and help her words make sense. "I mean, I really wanted you to know what it was like to be a

Christian, and I didn't want to scare you away from the faith or anything, so a lot of my own struggles I kept hidden. Like that PTSD stuff. I'm still a mess. You know that. At least, I think you know that. God hasn't healed me completely yet. I pray he does. I hope he does. It doesn't make sense to me how if the Bible says *ask and you shall receive*, I could ask him to take my flashbacks away and have him tell me no, he's not going to do that. I struggle with that one a lot. So maybe we're not going through the same kind of issues, but neither one of us has it figured out. Not even close."

"So, what exactly does that mean?" Willow asked. "Like, you get a flashback and start wondering if God exists? That doesn't sound like you."

"No, but I start to doubt if he's as powerful as he says he is. I mean, of course I know he is, but then I wonder why if he's all that powerful he doesn't just make my issues disappear? I've heard of people he's done that for. I know it's possible. So if he'd do it for someone else, why not me? I don't doubt he exists, but I do wonder if maybe it's my own lack of faith that's keeping him from answering my prayers."

Willow didn't say anything.

"I don't know if I'm making any sense right now. I'm probably just confusing you even more."

Willow sighed. "No, it's ok. It's good to hear I'm not the only one with those kinds of questions."

"I wish I had more answers for you," Kennedy admitted.

Willow offered a faint smile. "Maybe that's why they call it faith, right?"

Kennedy tried to smile back, but her heart ached for her friend. It wasn't supposed to be like this. Over Christmas break when Willow first started expressing an interest in Christianity, Kennedy had pictured the two of them bonding like sisters, taking their friendship to deeper levels. Willow's conversion was supposed to give Kennedy that deep Christian fellowship she'd always hoped to find in college. They could pray together at night, study the Bible together in the morning. It'd be like having a built-in accountability partner and prayer partner all rolled into one blissful friendship.

Instead, the two girls had drifted farther apart over the past few months. Willow was so careful about everything now, so worried about offending Kennedy or saying something wrong. If it wasn't about when to turn the lights out or who would be back to their dorm room when, the girls hardly talked at all.

"So, you're probably gonna tell me it was God who started the whole epidemic, just so I wouldn't go to New York and start partying again, right?"

Kennedy stared past Willow's shoulder at all the dishes that still needed to get washed and put away. "Well, I'm sure there's got to be more to it than that. If all he wanted to do was cancel your trip to New York, he could have done it in a lot of simpler ways."

"Like infecting me with Nipah?"

Kennedy wasn't sure if Willow was being sarcastic or not. "No, he doesn't work like that. It's not a punishment." She hoped she was speaking the truth. Didn't the Bible say Christians were no longer under God's wrath? But what about the other verses that talked about his discipline?

"It doesn't seem fair that a bunch of innocent people should catch a disease and die because I was about to go to New York and get involved in stuff I wasn't supposed to."

"No, God doesn't do it that way." Kennedy tried to think up a Bible verse that would prove her point. Where was Dominic when she needed him?

"What about those freaks ... I mean those evangelists like that Hopewell guy who gets up on TV and says you've just got to have faith and everything's going to work out? Or if you're sick or something and don't get better, it's because you've sinned. Isn't that why that one family stopped giving their son chemo? I mean, I guess I always assumed faith healers were just a bunch of quacks, but now that I'm saved, am I supposed to take what they say more seriously?"

Kennedy didn't pay much attention to preachers like that. Even Dominic, who believed more fervently in the power of prayer than anyone Kennedy had met, disagreed with that sort of prosperity gospel, or at least he disagreed with the way it was presented by the big-name televangelists. "No, for the most part I think I probably agree with you."

"So sickness isn't, like, some big punishment from God. That's what you're saying? That it doesn't mean you've sinned or something if you get sick?"

"I don't think so."

Willow let out a heavy sigh. "And what do you think about the whole Nipah thing, anyway? Not spiritually, just in general. Figure it'll get a lot worse?"

"I don't know." Kennedy didn't want to admit she'd been basically ignoring the entire epidemic, thinking until recently it was just another of her dad's overreactions.

"You think the kid's gonna be ok? If he was at that school ..."

Kennedy shook her head. She was pretty sure Woong was still engrossed in his *Princess Bride* reenactment, but she didn't want to risk him overhearing. The poor boy had lived through enough torment already before coming to the States. He didn't need another scare on his hands.

Kennedy stood up when her cell phone rang. "Hold on," she told Willow. "That's probably my dad freaking out again. I better get it before he has a heart attack or something."

She headed to the counter and glanced at the phone.

"Hello?"

"Kennedy." Sandy's voice on the other line was breathless.

Kennedy's gut tightened. "Yeah?"

"We're back in town, but something happened. Carl's not doing well. We're on our way to the ER at Providence right now."

"What is it?" Kennedy asked, trying to keep her voice from betraying her fears.

"I don't know. But please, would you find my journal, the one I keep up on the counter by the Bible and prayer box? A few pages in, you'll see the numbers for the St. Margaret's prayer chain. Could you call them, honey? I know it's a lot to ask. I think we have about fifteen names there. If you don't get a hold of them right away, just leave a message and ask them to call the people below them on the prayer chain when they get the chance."

"What should I tell them?" Kennedy pictured Carl's broad, smiling face. He was so strong. Of course, he could

77

afford to lose some weight. All that brawn and muscle that had made him a formidable Saints linebacker in his day had softened and filled out over time, but he was in perfect health for his age. In fact, he could easily pass as a decade or two younger. Kennedy had seen a picture of him and Sandy on their wedding day, and the only difference between then and now was that he'd gained forty or fifty extra pounds and traded a full head of hair for a pair of spectacles.

"I don't know what's going on, sweetheart, but you know Carl. He'd go visiting folks in the hospital every day of his life but wouldn't voluntarily step foot in one as a patient unless it was something pretty severe."

"Is it ..." Kennedy wasn't sure how to ask the question. Wasn't sure she wanted to know the answer. "Does it have anything to do with the epidemic?" She didn't speak over a whisper. She tried not to glance at Willow, who was offering her a sympathetic look from the dining room table.

Kennedy heard a noise in the background of Sandy's call. She thought she recognized Carl's voice but couldn't tell what was going on. Was he coughing? Crying out? Her throat seized up.

"Kennedy, I've got to go. Why don't you grab Woong and meet us here at Providence."

Kennedy had never heard so much fear in Sandy's voice before. She croaked out "Ok," but Sandy had already disconnected the call. Kennedy stared at the blank screen.

"Was that your pastor's wife?" Willow asked.

"Yeah, she's taking Carl to Providence right now. He's having some ..."

Willow cleared her throat loudly. "Well, hello. Sounded like you were having fun back there. Which *Princess Bride* character are you?"

"I'm the funny white-haired guy with the chocolate pill." Woong gave out a squeaky impression of Billy Crystal. "You better leave or I'll call the brute squad."

They both giggled. Thank God Willow was here to entertain Woong while he recited movie lines. Kennedy's brain was too stunned to do anything but stare at the cluttered counter.

"Hey," Willow asked, "what other movies do you like? Have you seen *The Avengers*?"

Woong frowned. "Only the cartoon ones. My mom won't let me watch the real thing."

"Well, do you have a favorite Avenger character?"

"Iron Man!" Woong answered excitedly.

"Do you have any Iron Man action figures?"

"Action what?"

"You know. Toys to play with. Toys that look like Iron Man."

"Oh, yeah. Wanna see?"

"Sure do. Why don't you go pick out your favorite from your room and bring it out here?" Willow turned to Kennedy as Woong sped down the hall. "What can I do to help?"

Kennedy pressed her fingertips against her temples. She had to focus. "Sandy has some people she wants me to call. People from the church. She's got the numbers in that journal over there." She pointed to the notebook. "And she said ..." Her voice caught for just a moment before she seized control of herself. "She said we should bring Woong and meet them at the hospital."

Willow stood up and grabbed the journal with the phone numbers. "Then that's what we're going to do." She walked down the hall and handed Kennedy her sweater. "Come on. Let's go."

"I don't have the car," Kennedy explained. "The youth pastor's borrowing it for the afternoon." For the first time, she thought about Nick and wondered why he hadn't returned the Honda earlier. She'd expected him back hours ago.

"Don't worry about that. We'll take mine. I'll drive and you can make those calls on the way. Please tell me you've kept your phone charged up this time."

Willow was only trying to lighten the mood. Kennedy's negligence in keeping her phone batteries charged was a constant source of teasing. But until she found out just what was wrong with Carl, there was no way she could find anything amusing.

"Hello. My name is Inigo Montoya." Woong rushed down the hall, holding a large Iron Man action figure and beaming proudly at Willow. "You killed my father. Prepare to die."

"That's wicked awesome," she exclaimed. "Hey, how old are you again?"

Woong shrugged. "I dunno."

"No, seriously. How old are you?"

"He really doesn't know," Kenny whispered in her ear.

Willow raised her penciled eyebrows. "Oh. Well, you're old enough to put on your shoes by yourself, right?"

Woong stared at his feet. "I'm already wearing my shoes."

"Look at that," Willow exclaimed. "Well, why don't you come out with me to my car, and when you're buckled in, you can put them on the right feet, ok?"

"Where are we going?" he asked. "I don't think my mom wants me going anywhere with strangers on account of some of them turning into bad guys, and you can never tell who the bad guys are just by looking at them, you know."

Willow smiled. "Your mom's right, and you're a very smart boy for remembering what she said. Kennedy's coming with us too, so that makes it all right, doesn't it?"

"I dunno." He glanced at Kennedy. "She's not a stranger to you, is she?"

Kennedy slipped on her new spring sandals and gave a pitiful attempt of a smile. "No, this is my good friend Willow. She's not a stranger."

Woong seemed appeased enough. "Where are we going?"

She wondered how much she should tell him. Before she knew herself what was going on, was it worth making him more scared? "We're going to visit your mom and dad."

"Wicked awesome!" Woong shouted and followed the girls out the door.

CHAPTER 9

Kennedy was only able to get a hold of six of the church members from Sandy's prayer chain list. She called them on the way to Providence, while Willow and Woong held a loud, lengthy conversation about their favorite Marvel heroes and villains. By the time they pulled into the hospital parking lot, Kennedy's insides were quivering like a glass of water left out in a Jurassic Park cafeteria table.

"You holding up?" Willow asked quietly as everyone unbuckled.

"I think so." Kennedy thought about her dad, thought about how a crowded emergency room was the last place he'd want her to visit in the middle of the Nipah outbreak, but what choice did she have? She turned to Willow. "You want to just drop us off here? We don't all have to go in."

"Isn't this the hospital?" Woong asked. "Is my dad visiting someone from the church? Did someone from St. Margaret's get sick? Wait, it's not the nipple disease, is it?"

Kennedy bit her lip so no one could see it tremble.

Willow reached out and gave her shoulder a reassuring squeeze. "I'll go in with you."

"You're not worried about catching anything?" Kennedy asked.

Willow shrugged. "How big of a hypocrite would I be if I were willing to go to New York City when there's been like twenty or thirty people who've died there, but I wouldn't step into a hospital to help a friend?"

Kennedy returned her roommate's smile and this time didn't have to fake it. "Thanks."

"Hey, that's what I'm here for."

They headed toward the emergency room entrance. Kennedy wished she'd brought more practical shoes than her little spring sandals. She also realized she'd left her backpack and Germ-X back at the Lindgrens' home. Oh, well. Providence had several sanitation stations. Maybe they'd have masks too. That way, if her dad ever found out she'd been here, she could at least tell him she'd taken every possible precaution, or at least every reasonable one.

"You have to be really careful when we get in," she told Woong as they entered through the automatic doors. "Don't put your hands on anything, and try not to touch your face, ok?"

"Why not?"

Kennedy didn't have the stamina to give him a well thought out, scientific response. "Just be careful, all right?" She felt like Forrest Gump's mother, repeating the same couple phrases over and over again.

Once they entered the ER, Woong frowned. "Hey, where's my dad? This is usually the room where he visits people and prays with them. That reminds me, my head hurts. If I ask my dad to pray about it, think it'll go away?"

"Your dad's in a different room this time," Kennedy told him. "In fact, buddy, your dad's here because ..."

"Oh, baby boy, come over here, little pumpkin." Sandy burst out of a doorway and bustled over to Woong, her long, flowered skirt rustling round her legs until she reached her son and smothered him in kisses.

Woong squirmed in her arms.

"I missed you so much, darling. Are you ok? Your daddy wants to see you. Kennedy, thank you so much for bringing him here. The doctors are doing tests right now, but they said I could bring him back. Were you a good boy for Miss Kennedy?" she asked. "You didn't give her too much of a hard time? Your daddy's been asking for you, honey. He'll be so happy to know you came to see him."

And with that, Sandy ushered Woong past the nurse who held open a door labeled *authorized personnel only.*

Kennedy and Willow looked at each other.

"So do we wait or head out?" Willow asked.

Kennedy glanced around. The ER wasn't overcrowded, but it was more sick people than she was comfortable sharing space with if she didn't have to. "Maybe I'll text Sandy real quick and ask." She pulled out her cell.

"Yeah, what's wrong with your pastor, anyway? I didn't want to ask in the car. Didn't want to worry the boy."

"Me either. But I have no idea what's going on. Sandy didn't really say anything, just that it seemed serious if it meant he's here at the ER. He's not that fond of doctors, actually."

Willow glanced around. "Can't blame him."

Kennedy stared at the text on her screen. "Well, that was easy enough. Sandy said she'll keep Woong here for now, so I guess that means we don't have to stick around."

Willow shrugged. "All right. Hey, wanna hit L'Aroma Bakery? They've got this new eggless quiche I've been dying to try."

"I better not. My dad ..."

Willow smiled. "Say no more. Time to go sequester ourselves again?"

"I guess so." They started to walk toward the exit. Kennedy cleared her throat. "Thanks for coming with me."

"No problem."

"I really mean it. That was … Well, it was nice not having to drive Woong by myself. I was pretty worried."

"I could tell. Hey, can I ask you a question?

"Sure."

"It's about your PTSD."

"Oh." Kennedy took a deep breath. Good. No choppiness. "Go ahead."

"I was wondering if you think you're …"

"Kennedy!" The voice behind them made both girls stop and turn around.

"Dominic!"

"What are you both doing here?" he asked. Concern laced his words. "Everything ok?"

"We just brought Woong over to see Carl," Kennedy told him, hoping Dominic could give more details about her pastor's condition.

Dominic frowned. "Carl? Is he here visiting someone?"

Kennedy bit her lip. "No, he's here as a patient. You didn't know?"

"No." Dominic glanced behind him once. "I got called here on different business."

"Everything ok?" she asked.

"Oh." He cleared his throat awkwardly. "You know.

Work stuff." Why wouldn't he meet her eyes? "So, you're taking off then?" he asked.

Kennedy tried to read his muted expression. She hated the way he couldn't talk to her about his job as a police chaplain. She understood the need for privacy, but she was his girlfriend, after all.

"Yeah, we're heading out right now." Was he trying to rush her out the door? What was going on?

He looked relieved. "Ok, well, I'm glad we bumped into each other."

Kennedy paused. "Are you ok?"

Dominic was looking over her shoulder. "Hmm."

She didn't know if that was an affirmative sound or not. She reached out and touched his arm. "What's wrong?"

Something beeped, and he grabbed his pager out of his pocket. "I'm sorry, I've got to run. I'll call you tonight." He took off at a sprint.

Willow chuckled. "Wow. When he said he had to run, I didn't think he meant it quite so literally."

Kennedy stared after him. What was that all about?

Willow planted on a chipper expression that clashed glaringly against Kennedy's current mood. "So, we've got a whole week ahead of us, no kids to watch, and nowhere to go. Sounds like the perfect recipe for a little bit of fun."

Willow was right. This was spring break, after all. Even if the stupid epidemic meant they were trapped indoors, at least they could have a good time together. Board games. Movies. They'd find ways to keep each other from getting stir-crazy. And even though they were in the midst of an epidemic, maybe they could stop by the gas station on the way home and pick up a gallon of ice cream. What her dad didn't know couldn't hurt him.

"All right, let's head out." Even though she felt bad for her roommate, she was thankful the New York trip had been cancelled. If you had to sit around hiding from a horrific virus, might as well do it with someone you enjoyed spending time with.

"Sounds like a plan." Willow rubbed Kennedy encouragingly on the back. Kennedy tried not to think of her strange run-in with Dominic. He was always serious at work, but that's because he did his job so well, felt so much compassion and empathy for the families he prayed with and assisted. She knew he'd keep his word, and they'd talk more tonight. Until then, she and Willow could afford a day of fun.

"Hold on." Kennedy stopped at the hand sanitizing station by the exit. "All right." She wiped the excess lotion on her pants legs and smiled at her roommate. "Let's go."

The automatic doors swung open as an alarm blared across the hospital PA system.

"This is a hospital-wide code 241. Repeat. Code 241, hospital wide."

Kennedy and Willow stopped and glanced at each other as a security officer came up behind them. "Excuse me. I need you both to have a seat in the lobby." He stepped in front of them, blocking their exit.

"What's going on?" Kennedy asked.

"Just have a seat." He nodded toward the chairs in the waiting area as the announcer on the PA system repeated the encrypted announcement.

Kennedy and Willow slowly made their way to two empty seats. Kennedy's open-toed sandals, cute as they were, pinched against the sides of her feet. Another security officer closed the doors that connected the ER to the main hospital then stood there, mute and expressionless. Across from her, a middle-aged man coughed into his coat sleeve. A mother held her small son against her chest and adjusted his face mask to cover his mouth and nose. A baby cried somewhere behind her, but Kennedy didn't turn around to look.

"What do you think's going on?" Willow asked.

Kennedy made a valiant attempt to control the terror

swirling around in her gut. She visualized herself compressing it into a tiny, infinitesimally small singularity, burying it along with all her other fears and anxieties.

"I don't have the slightest idea."

CHAPTER 10

Kennedy tried calling Dominic's cell five different times. Either he didn't have it on or something kept him from answering.

She went up to the nurses' station and stood in line behind ten other people until the petite triage nurse finally told her that a Code 241 meant no one could enter or leave the building.

"For how long?"

"I can't say."

"What are they keeping us here for?"

"I really don't know."

Did she know anything? "I came in to check on a friend. Carl Lindgren," she explained. "Is there any way I can go back and see him?"

She shook her head. "I'm sorry. Right now I can't let you back there. Not with the hospital on lockdown."

"Is this a quarantine or something?"

"I really can't say. I'm sorry."

"Is it about the Nipah virus?"

"I'm afraid I don't know any more than you do. I'm sorry."

I'm sorry. I'm sorry. I'm sorry.

Kennedy was sick of it.

"Would you like a sanitation mask?" the nurse asked.

"Sure. Actually, can I have two? I'm here with a friend." At least they'd be waiting out this lockdown in style.

"No problem."

Kennedy plodded back to her seat and handed her roommate a mask.

"No answers?" Willow asked.

"Nothing."

And so they waited. Willow wanted to play Scrabble on their phones, but Kennedy's battery was running low.

Willow sighed dramatically. "This stinks."

"Yeah."

"What's the Bible have to say about stuff like this?"

Kennedy had grown used to Willow insulting religion for so long at first she thought she was joking. Her eyes alone proved Willow's question was earnest.

"I don't know. I guess there's Romans." She shifted in her seat. It was uncomfortable the way the mask made her talk so much louder than normal to keep her words from getting muffled. "It says all things work together for good for those who love God."

"Yeah? Like we're here on a hospital lockdown, and while we're stuck here, I'm gonna end up meeting the love of my life? That sort of good?"

Kennedy smiled. "No, it could just mean he's teaching us patience." Wasn't there a verse like that in James? Or maybe it was one of the Peters. A verse about being thankful for your trials because they mature your faith. Why couldn't she have done a better job memorizing Scripture and keeping track of all those references?

Willow crossed her arms. "I could think of less painful ways to learn patience if you asked me."

Kennedy glanced around. At least hospitals were interesting places to people-watch if you found yourself stuck in one. Across from her, a toddler in an adult-sized mask was sleeping on his mother's lap. His legs were curled up until he was no bigger than a beach ball, and his hands were tucked down by his knees. He looked almost cherubic. A middle-aged man was talking to the security guard in front of the ER entrance. Kennedy couldn't tell if he was animated because he was angry or worried.

She looked behind her. Nipah was one of those diseases that made people contagious a few days before they developed symptoms. How many people weren't sick now but would be by the end of the week? Would Kennedy be among them? How long was this lockdown going to take?

"So what else does God have to say about this sort of stuff?" Willow asked.

Kennedy had to get used to her roommate taking spiritual matters seriously for a change. "Well, I guess he tells us not to be anxious. Have you read the verse about the birds? He says that not even a sparrow falls to the ground apart from God's will and that we're worth a lot more in God's sight than they are."

"So if we die of some horrific disease, it's only because God wanted us to?"

Kennedy sighed. "I guess that just about sums it up."

They were silent for a few minutes before Willow took off her mask. "Can they really keep us here like this?" she asked in a whisper. "I mean, legally and stuff?"

Kennedy shrugged. "I guess if they have a good enough reason."

Willow shook her head. "This country is so messed up. You know, this whole Nipah virus probably already has some homeopathic cure, but they're not telling us about it because it doesn't profit the big corporations. It all comes down to money in the end. Like that couple who nearly got sent to jail because they refused chemo for their son." She shook her head. "Wicked insane. What do you think?"

The question caught Kennedy off guard. "About chemotherapy?" Her mind was still reeling after her brief encounter with Dominic and the mysterious lockdown. She couldn't even remember when they started talking about cancer.

"No, about sickness in general. And medicine. I mean, aren't there a lot of religious folks who deny medical care because they just assume God's going to heal them and that's that? Is that in the Bible or something?"

"No, I mean, it's just ..." Why couldn't she give a straight answer?

"But what about how Jesus healed so many people in ancient times? Is that something he still can do today? Or does he just leave it up to the doctors and nurses now?"

Kennedy knew Dominic would have a better answer for her. They'd talked about the power of prayer and healing before. Dominic knew a little girl who'd been hit by a drunk driver. The doctors thought she was completely brain-dead, but Dominic and the parents prayed over her, and within a few hours she woke up from her coma and eventually made a full recovery that left the medical community baffled. Of course God could still heal people in miraculous ways, but that still didn't explain how it worked or how he picked which Christians got divine intervention and which didn't.

"Well, it's definitely possible for God to heal someone," she began, but Willow's questions compounded too fast before she could answer any of them thoroughly.

"And what about those Christians who say God will cure anyone who has enough faith? Like Cameron Hopewell or whatever his name is, strutting around on TV shouting at people to be healed. Makes it out like if you go to a doctor or something you're not trusting God enough. Tells diabetics to go off their meds, that sort of thing. Is there something to that?"

"No, I mean, there's nothing wrong with seeking medical treatment. It's just ..." Why was she always fumbling her words like this?

"So it's not wrong to go to a doctor and take medicine."

"Not at all."

"But what about the dangerous drugs with all their horrible side effects and things like that? What's the Bible got to say about those?"

Kennedy didn't have a ready answer and would be surprised if any of the theologians in her contacts list would fare better on that one. "I guess it's up to each person to make the choice that seems best to them." It was a cop-out, but it was all she had to offer.

They were silent for a while longer. Kennedy hadn't stopped worrying about Carl. She wished she knew what was going on.

Willow had pulled the mask back over her face. She leaned back in her seat and asked, "So what are we supposed to do now?"

"Do?"

"Yeah. You know. Do. It's a verb. Means take action."

What did Willow expect? That Kennedy could snap her fingers and bring an end to the lockdown? That she could call up Dominic and tell him she and Willow wanted to go home? "I don't know."

"Well, what would your pastor or his wife do if they were out here? What do you think they're doing right now?"

"I'm sure they're back there praying together." Kennedy took a small slice of comfort at the thought of the Lindgrens' strong faith, but her emotions were clouded by her fears for Carl's health. Why hadn't Sandy given her more information? Kennedy should call, but her battery was nearly dead after all those messages she'd delivered to the prayer chain on the way to Providence. She'd seen enough hospital dramas with her mom to know a real quarantine could last several days. How long did it take for Nipah symptoms to develop? Where was her dad's WebMD recital when she needed it?

"So what is it they're praying for exactly? Do you just pray you won't get sick and then everything works out? I feel like a lot more Christians would be healthy if it were that simple."

Kennedy shook her head. "No, it's not that simple." She knew all too well there were some sicknesses you just couldn't pray away. How it all worked was a mystery to her and would probably remain so until the day she died.

Willow nudged her softly in the ribs. "Ok, so your pastor and his wife are praying. Doesn't that mean we should be doing it too?"

"Praying for what?"

"You're the one with all those years of Sunday-school-girl living under your belt. Why don't you tell me?"

Kennedy glanced around the crowded waiting room. "You want to pray right here? Like just drop our heads and start talking to God?"

She shrugged. "Unless you've got a better idea."

"No. Not really."

"Then let's have at it." Willow folded her hands and bowed her head like she did the night she prayed to be saved.

Kennedy shot one more nervous glance around and then

decided if her brand-new baby Christian of a roommate could pray out in public, she could too. She pulled down her mask so she wouldn't have to feel like she was yelling and took in a deep breath, wondering how to start. How did you pray in a situation like this? What was there to say other than *your will be done*? Isn't that what was going to happen anyway? So why pray for anything else? When it came right down to it, why bother to pray at all?

To Kennedy's surprise, Willow started first. "Dear Jesus, hey thanks so much that we got Woong here in time to see his dad before they locked the doors. We hope that Carl's just fine. And please tell the hospital folks to let us leave. If people here are sick, we hope that you make them well. I guess that's all. Amen."

She looked up and raised an eyebrow at Kennedy. "You gonna pray, too?"

Kennedy unfolded her hands. "No, I think you covered everything."

Willow frowned. "Felt pretty short."

"I'm sure it was fine." She couldn't explain why her throat had chosen now of all times to threaten to close in on her and cut off her breath. Or why her heart decided to start racing as fast as the police officer had to drive that bus in *Speed*.

She stood up, thankful that her muscles could still

support her weight. She was dizzy, but she could make it to the bathroom. She grabbed her phone. "Excuse me. I'll be back in just a sec."

Willow acted like she was about to stand up. "Where are you going? Something wrong?"

Kennedy held out her hand. "Yeah. Don't worry. I've just ... I have to pee. I'll be back soon."

"Sheesh, woman. You'd think you had a bladder the size of a ping-pong ball."

Kennedy didn't reply. She just hoped she'd make it to the bathroom before panic took complete control over her body.

Panting, choking, half-sobbing, she floundered almost blindly into the restroom. She sank onto one of the toilets, too paralyzed to even worry about germs. She fumbled with her phone, praying she wouldn't drop it into the bowl.

Please be there. Please be there.

She didn't bother to think about what time it might be right now in Yanji. There was only one voice she needed to hear.

"Kennedy? Everything all right?"

She sniffed loudly, thankful there wasn't anyone else in the bathroom with her.

"Daddy?" Her voice cracked, but she didn't care.

"What is it, princess? What's wrong?"

She bit her lip, praying for her cell phone to hold its charge for at least a few more minutes.

"What's wrong?" her dad repeated.

"You watching the news?" she asked in a shaky whisper.

"I've got Channel 2 up right here. Looks like there's something happening over at one of the hospitals. Providence? Is that near you?"

Snot dribbled down her nose. Tears raced down her cheeks. Her breath caught twice before she could hiccup out the next words.

"I'm here, Dad. I'm at the hospital right now. I'm in the middle of a lockdown."

CHAPTER 11

"Kennedy. Princess." Her father's voice was authoritative. Not a trace of panic. Not a trace of impatience as Kennedy wheezed and choked and tried desperately to keep from suffocating in the cramped bathroom stall. "Where are you right now? Where exactly?"

"In the bathroom," she managed to reply.

"Not good enough. What part of the hospital are you in?"

"The ER."

"What are you doing there?" Her dad spoke to her as if she were a preschooler practicing her animal sounds. *And what does the cow say?*

She sniffed. Something about her dad's authoritative tone grounded her. She tried to cling to whatever strength he was offering her from the other side of the planet. "Carl ... Something was wrong with Carl. Sandy called and said I should bring Woong here to see him."

"And what are Carl's symptoms? Does he have a fever? Swelling in the brain? Aches?"

"I don't know." Kennedy wiped her nose on a wad of scratchy toilet paper.

"Ok. So where's Woong? Is he there with you?"

"No. He's with his parents. We were just about to leave when they shut the doors." Her lungs spasmed as she tried to take in a pained breath. "We were just a foot away from the exit."

"Who's we?" her dad demanded. "Who are you there with?"

"Willow. I came here with Willow."

"She's not sick, is she?"

"No, we're both fine. But we're stuck here. And they're not giving us any answers or telling us when we'll be able to go."

"That's all right." How could her dad lie to her like that? This was the guy who was freaking out when some unnamed 72-year-old pig farmer in Bangladesh came down with the Nipah virus. He'd freaked out way back then, and now here she was, stuck in a hospital in the middle of an outbreak about to reach the level of global pandemic, and he was telling her she was fine.

"I don't know what's going on. They haven't told us anything."

"Is it the Nipah?" he asked. "Have you been exposed?"

"I don't know. I just came here so Woong could be with his dad." Tears slipped down her cheeks. She couldn't erase her brain's projected images of Carl, weak and sick in a faded hospital gown, faintly holding his son's hand. What was wrong with him? Would he be ok? She could almost endure the thought of being locked here if she knew he was all right.

"What about the other patients in the ER? What kind of symptoms have you seen there?"

"I don't know. I don't know anything." That's what made this entire scenario so unbearable. The uncertainty. When would they get released? What if they weren't sick yet but would catch the disease while they were all shut up in here like the prisoners in *Shawshank Redemption*?

"Ok. Well, hospitals get locked down for all kinds of reasons. Is it just the ER or the whole thing that's closed?"

"I think it's the whole thing."

"You think?"

She felt the edge of annoyance creep through her veins. Being angry at her dad was preferable to feeling so panicked and terrified. "How should I know? Nobody's telling us anything."

"Just calm down. Don't get so worked up if you can help it."

Don't get so worked up. He was the perfect person to tell

her that. Mr. The-World-is-Ending. *Thanks, Dad. That's really helpful.*

"Take a deep breath," he instructed.

As if Kennedy weren't trying.

"Ok, listen to me. If this lockdown has something to do with the Nipah virus, if they're worried about infection, they're going to set up triage stations. Figure out who needs to be quarantined, who needs to be isolated, who may or may not have been exposed. That's what's going to happen if they think there's been some sort of outbreak. Understand?"

"Yeah."

"And you know how fast people end up getting sick, right? Perfectly fine and then bam, they're too sick to walk in half an hour's time. So you got to stay alert. Keep your eye on all the other patients there. Avoid getting close to anyone."

"I know." She wished she'd listened to her dad sooner, wished she hadn't ignored all his earlier advice.

"And I know Nipah's scary stuff, but remember it might not be that. There are plenty of other reasons hospitals go into lockdown."

"Like what?"

"Could be anything. Terrorist attack. Security breach. Armed gunman."

Did her dad honestly expect any of this information to be helpful?

"What you want to do is stay close to the people you think are in charge. Look around. Position yourself near the ones who are most likely to have the answers. And then just wait it out. Nearly all of these situations get resolved in less than twenty-four hours."

It was confirmed. Her dad would never be invited to give a motivational speech anywhere.

"Ok." At least she could breathe a little easier now. At least she knew what to look for. If this was some sort of quarantine, they'd separate them into groups. Isolate the sickest. Keep the healthy from getting exposed.

"Listen. Who do you know that you could call? Someone who might know what's going on? What about that journalist friend you've got? Do you have his number?"

"I don't remember." She didn't want to admit her phone was just a quarter of a bar away from dying. It had already beeped at her once.

"Think of people you know who might be able to tell you what's going on. Keep your phone right next to you. Don't waste your charge on games or anything like that. You never know how long this sort of thing will take to get resolved."

"All right." She was only listening to his words with half her mental energy. With the rest, she was begging God to keep the phone working until they were through with their conversation.

"I'm going to let you go now, princess. I'll call my lawyer friend. See if Jefferson knows anything about what's going on."

Kennedy couldn't figure out what information a Worcester attorney would have about a hospital lockdown, but she didn't ask. Maybe her dad just needed to feel useful. Feel like he was taking some sort of proactive measures.

Maybe she was more like him than she cared to admit.

"I love you, baby girl. You know that, right?"

"I love you too, Daddy."

"You take care now. And save your phone battery. I'll text you if I find out anything."

"Ok."

"Stay safe. Be smart."

"I will."

"Ok. Love you."

"You, too."

She sniffed and stared at the phone, thankful her battery had lasted through the entire conversation. She should write down her dad's number before it completely died. That way she could call him on Willow's phone if she needed to.

God, I just want to get out of here.

At least her breathing had calmed down. She wasn't hyperventilating anymore. She could do this. Walk back out to Willow. Give a smile. Pretend like everything was ok.

But was that what she should do? If Willow was open with her own struggles and doubts, shouldn't Kennedy try to be at least somewhat transparent? Then again, it's not like she was keeping her PTSD a secret. They'd talked about it just a few seconds before the lockdown.

No, Kennedy was doing what she needed to do. Get through the day without turning into a complete mess, a psychological puddle too pathetic to do anything. She just had to keep on functioning. That's all the victory she could expect at a time like this.

One minute at a time.

She went to the sink and washed her face, studying herself in the mirror to see if her eyes would betray her recent tears.

She jumped when her phone rang.

"Hello?"

"Kennedy, it's Dominic."

He cut her off when she started to ask about a dozen different questions at once.

"Listen to me. Listen very carefully. You might be in danger. You and Willow need to get out of the ER and meet me at the …"

She pressed the phone harder against her ear as if that would make her to hear better. "What? Where'd you go? What did you just say?"

Silence.

"Dominic?"

She stared at her phone.

Completely dead.

Kennedy bit her lip and hurried out of the bathroom.

It didn't matter anymore who could tell that she'd been crying.

ALANA TERRY

CHAPTER 12

"Ok, just calm down," Willow whispered, "and tell me exactly what he said."

Kennedy tried to keep her voice low so the other people in the waiting room couldn't overhear. "He said we might not be safe in the ER, and we should go meet him somewhere."

"Where?"

"I don't know. I lost the call before he could tell me."

"So call him back."

"My phone's dead."

Willow pulled her cell out of her purse. "Then use mine."

"I don't know his number."

Willow sighed. "Ok, well, let's think through it then. If he said the ER wasn't safe, then maybe there's somewhere else we could go."

"Yeah, but what about the security guards? They're not letting anyone get anywhere."

"So maybe we just ask."

111

"You can't just walk up to a guard in the middle of a lockdown and say, 'Hey, I need to find my boyfriend. He's in another part of the hospital and I don't know where, but can you let me get past so I can try to find him?' It doesn't work like that."

Kennedy was sulking, but she didn't care. If God wanted her to be a good example of spiritual maturity for her roommate, he needed to stop throwing her into these situations where her life was constantly in danger.

Willow didn't respond. At first, Kennedy thought she was just being moody too, but then she noticed her staring somewhere past Kennedy's shoulder.

"What are you looking at?"

"Holy cr … I mean, *holy cow*. Don't turn around right now, but some guy with gorgeous hair just walked into the waiting room."

Kennedy rolled her eyes, but something about seeing her roommate fawning over a man made her feel a little better. Some things didn't change. Even in the midst of a hospital lockdown, life went on.

It always would.

"Man, you should see him. No, don't turn yet, he's looking here. Oh my L … I mean, *oh man*. He's walking this way. He's looking right at me. He's coming straight over here." Willow ran her hands frantically over her magenta highlights.

"Hey, Kennedy. What are you doing here?"

"You mean you actually know him?" Willow hissed.

Kennedy turned around. "Oh, hi, Nick." She glanced at the large bandage on his head and momentarily forgot how big a fool her roommate was making of herself. "What happened to you? Are you ok?"

He let out a jocular laugh that carried through the entire waiting room and pointed at his bandage. "Oh, yeah. Got this defending some little old lady at the grocery store."

He sat down and stretched out his hand to Willow. "Hi, I'm Nick."

Willow stared for several seconds until Kennedy wondered if she'd forgotten her own name. "This is Willow," she answered for her. "She's my roommate."

"Hi, Willow."

Her hand was still in Nick's. "Oh. My. Goodness. That *hair*."

Nick laughed and pulled his hand away. "Oh, that. Yeah. I get that a lot."

"It's so long." Willow reached out her hand but stopped. "Can I? I mean, may I ..."

Nick shrugged. "Sure. Go ahead."

Willow picked up one of his dreads and ran her fingers all the way down to the tip. "That is the most wicked awesome thing I've seen in my entire life."

"What are you doing here?" Kennedy asked.

Willow still had his hair in her hand. "Yeah, what was that you said about a little old lady? Was that just a joke?"

"No. I'm dead serious." Nick unzipped his coat.

"Good grief." Willow stared. "Does that shirt make you a Christian?"

Nick chuckled. "No, I'm pretty sure only God can do that."

"Then does it mean you're a Christian?" Willow stared at the praying stick figure on Nick's chest.

"Nick's the youth pastor at Carl and Sandy's church," Kennedy told her.

"Oh. My. Goodness."

Kennedy was certain that beneath that sanitation mask, Willow's mouth was hanging wide open. "So what happened to you?" Kennedy asked again.

"Well, I went to go get groceries at Rory's, and like I told you earlier, nearly everything was gone. But they had a few things left, and I got my basket filled, but there was this little old lady. I mean, she probably wasn't even five foot tall. She had gotten the last few cans of chili beans. And these two thugs, I kid you not, they knocked her over just to get at her shopping basket. So I jumped in and ..." He shrugged and pointed to his bandaged forehead. "Ten stitches and a possible minor concussion later, here I am. Sorry I didn't get the car back to you on time."

"That's ok," Kennedy assured him.

"You were so heroic," Willow breathed.

Nick shrugged again. "Yeah, well, you should see the other guys."

"Really?" Willow asked. "Are they that bad off?"

"Who? The other guys? No, they walked away without a scratch." He grinned broadly. "But at least the little old lady got her chili beans."

Kennedy hadn't realized until now how nearly everyone in the waiting room was staring at them. Had they been talking that loudly? She'd been so amused watching her roommate's reaction to meeting Nick that she'd almost forgotten for a moment that they were in the middle of a lockdown.

Apparently, Nick was even more oblivious and kept chatting away. "What about you two? Everything ok here?" He pointed to his face. "What's up with the masks?"

Kennedy didn't even know where to begin explaining everything. "We were just bringing Woong here to see Carl."

"Carl? Isn't he still away with Sandy?"

"Not anymore. They cut their trip short when school got cancelled, then on the way home Sandy called and said she was bringing him here."

Nick's face dropped. "Why? What's wrong?"

Kennedy shrugged. "Wish I knew."

"Is it serious?"

"I don't know any more than that."

"So you two are just staying here until he gets out?"

"No," Kennedy answered. "We were on our way out when the lockdown started."

"Lockdown?" Nick glanced around the waiting room, apparently taking in the security guards near all the doors for the first time.

"You didn't hear?" Kennedy asked.

He chuckled nervously. "Truth be told, I don't handle needles all that well. I didn't really exactly pass out, but I'm not sure how with it I was while they were stitching me up."

Willow reached out and rubbed the top of his knee. "You poor thing. That's terrible."

Nick sighed melodramatically. "So what's going on then? What's this lockdown thing all about?"

"Nobody knows for sure," Willow piped up. She seemed eager to be the one leading the discussion for a change. "We think it might have something to do with …"

Kennedy had been distracted watching Willow and Nick's interactions and hadn't noticed the security officer coming up behind her. She had no idea he was there until he cleared his throat and tapped her on the shoulder.

"Excuse me, Miss."

"Yes?" She turned around. What was wrong? Were they in trouble for talking about the lockdown?

"Are you Kennedy Stern?"

Her stomach dropped as if she were in freefall on a rollercoaster. How did he know her?

"Yes," she answered tentatively. Her face heated up with the certainty that everyone in the waiting room was staring at her.

The security officer kept his voice low. "I need you to come with me, please."

"Is something wrong?" She stood up. "What's this all about?"

"Follow me," he repeated.

Kennedy didn't look back but knew that if she did, she'd see the worried glances of Willow and Nick following her as she shuffled behind the man in uniform and headed out of the ER.

CHAPTER 13

"Where are we going?" Kennedy's voice was timid. Afraid. At least she could breathe. Everything would be just fine as long as she kept on breathing.

Please, Jesus ...

"Just come with me." The security guard walked several paces ahead. Kennedy had to scurry to keep up. Why had she worn her little heeled sandals and not something more practical? Then again, when she left the Lindgrens', she'd only been thinking about making it to Providence fast. She hadn't stopped to worry about shoes fit for racing down empty hospital corridors.

"Is everything ok?" What kind of a stupid question was that? Nothing was ok. That's what happens when you're stuck in a hospital lockdown in the middle of a horrific epidemic. Why hadn't she taken her dad more seriously? Why had she breezed through the past few weeks taking her health for granted, refusing to think of all those people getting infected?

Folks were dying. Not just in far-off reaches of the globe. In New York. Florida. Right in her backyard in Boston itself. The Nipah virus didn't care if you were young or old, strong or weak. It didn't pay any attention to your medical history, your immunization record.

Kennedy was the queen of germophobes. Did her little bottle of Germ-X delude her into thinking she'd march through this whole epidemic unscathed?

She thought about different outbreaks she'd studied in history class. The black plague. More than decimated the world's population. Typhoid Mary. Infecting scores of individuals before doctors forced her into quarantine. Lived completely alone for decades before she finally died of pneumonia. More recently there'd been SARS, swine flu ... Kennedy had heard about all of those but never knew anyone who actually got sick from any of them.

Maybe that's where her little bubble of perceived invincibility came from. She'd never been seriously ill. Of course, there were all the typical childhood conditions. Colds. Stomach viruses. An ear infection or two. She'd had chicken pox, though she'd been so young she had no memories of it. Is that why she assumed she could blitz through this whole Nipah scare without having to worry herself about it?

She glanced at the hallways lined with closed doors, wondering how far she'd have to go before she'd learn what she was doing here. Was she infected? Did they suspect she was a carrier? Had Woong's teacher tested positive for Nipah? Were they quarantining everyone who was possibly exposed? How long would they keep her here? And what about Willow? Had she put her roommate in danger?

She hated hospitals. Hated the bleached, antiseptic smells that only vaguely masked the odor of vomit and blood and bodily fluids. She hated the way hospital air made her skin crawl, as if every single germ in a ten-foot radius swarmed her like a mob of hungry mosquitoes. It was ironic, really. Before starting college, she'd pictured herself in that white gown, stethoscope hanging from her neck like a mantle, walking stately from one needy patient to another. Now she just hoped she could make it down a single hallway without turning into a hyperventilating mess.

Her counselor said that maybe Kennedy's academic drive was related to her trauma experiences. That maybe she threw herself into her studies to combat how helpless she'd felt watching a young girl nearly hemorrhage to death on a grimy bathroom floor at the start of her freshman year. It sounded logical, but he hadn't met Kennedy before the PTSD. She'd been like this for as long as she could remember. Always been a control freak. An overachiever. With or without the panic attacks, she'd always pushed herself past her breaking point. Anything for the grade. For the sense of accomplishment. That's how she'd gotten into Harvard's early acceptance medical program to begin with.

She was destined to become one of the nation's top physicians. Except she couldn't stand five minutes in a hospital.

Who ever said God didn't have a sense of humor?

If anything, her disdain for hospitals started over a decade ago, at her grandmother's bedside as she lay dying from lung cancer. Kennedy had been so young. So naïve. So certain that what the Bible and her Sunday school teachers always told her was true. If she prayed, God would answer.

And so she'd prayed. So fervently. With that impossible to imitate faith of a child. A child who foolishly believed that if she trusted hard enough, God would always give her what she asked for. It's not like she was praying for a pony to ride or a castle to live in. She just wanted her grandma to be healed. To be able to go back to her own home. Enjoy her evenings with *Wheel of Fortune* and *Jeopardy* and her cans of plain black beans she heated up for dinner. To be there every Christmas and every summer break in that beautifully quaint little cottage in upstate New York. Far from the city, from traffic. Kennedy's perfect little refuge. Where she'd catch dragonflies in the summer and race her dad down giant sledding hills in the winter.

All she'd wanted was for Grandma to stay alive. It wasn't fair she'd gotten lung cancer in the first place. She'd never smoked a day in her life. Hated cigarettes. But still came down with the dreaded disease after spending forty years married to a chain-smoking addict.

In the end, it's what killed her. Killed her in spite of Kennedy's prayers. In spite of Kennedy's perfect, childlike faith. In spite of all the Bible promises Kennedy read and claimed and called her own.

Grandma still died, but not until after six months of torment. Six months of torture. With her hair falling out in clumps, her entire body hooked up to tubes and machines that reminded Kennedy of some scene from *Star Trek: First Contact*. No wonder there were those parents who refused chemo for their kids. Six months while the medicine ravaged her grandma's body. Poisoned her blood. It shrunk one of the tumors for a few months. Enough time for Kennedy to assume her prayers really had worked.

Until a routine checkup showed the tumor had grown. And spread. And by then, there was nothing to do but make hospice arrangements.

And still Kennedy held onto faith that God would heal her grandma. Held onto that faith until the morning her grandma died, surrounded by family, covered in tubes, her body shrunken to nearly half her pre-diagnosis weight.

Is it any wonder Kennedy hated hospitals?

She let out her breath. This line of thinking wasn't going to get her anywhere. *Come on.* She gave herself the best pep talk she could muster. *Think about something else and snap yourself out of this.* The last thing the guard needed was a hysterical basket case on his hands.

She bit her lip, focusing on the pain it caused. She glanced around her, desperately hoping her eyes would land on something to ground her. Something to snap her brain back to the present. Her counselor had given her clear instructions when she felt a panic attack rising up in her chest. Name four things you can see. Four things you can hear. Focus on her senses, not on her irrational fear.

It made perfect sense on paper. Harder to do when your lungs have already decided to seize shut on you. Harder to do when your breath is so short and choppy your brain's overcome with dizziness until you're certain you're about to suffocate. When your heart's racing so fast you wonder if you're about to become the first sophomore in the history of Harvard University to die from cardiac arrest.

She bit her lip even harder when the officer unlocked a small room at the farthest end of the impossibly long hallway. Her thoughts flashed back once more to Typhoid Mary, locked up for decades to keep from infecting anyone around her.

That couldn't be what was happening to her. She was a citizen. She had rights. Her dad knew lawyers ...

"Kennedy? Thank God they found you."

At the sound of the welcomed voice, she rushed toward Dominic who held out his arms to her.

"It's ok," he whispered. "You're safe here."

CHAPTER 14

"What's going on?" Kennedy had lost track of how many times by now Dominic had seen her cry. He'd seen when her panic was at its worst. She was too relieved to find him here to feel embarrassed. It was one of Dominic's greatest strengths, what made him such an effective chaplain. He had such a calming presence. Even when he wasn't whispering his powerful prayers over her, Kennedy got the sense he was interceding for her anyway. The impression that when she was with him, her spirit and body were surrounded by an extra layer of heavenly protection.

"It's ok." He stroked her hair and then led her to a small couch. She glanced around and realized they were in the same small conference room where she'd met him a full year ago.

"What's going on?" she asked again.

"Shh." He patted her hand and sat down beside her. "I can't stay long. I just wanted to make sure you got out of the ER."

Kennedy glanced at the door and discovered the security guard who led her here was already gone. "What about everyone else? Willow's still there."

"It's going to be ok." He was sitting next to her. So close. She leaned her forehead on his shoulder, wishing she could stay like this forever. Or at least until the lockdown ended and everyone was able to go home safely.

"What about my friends? Are they going to get exposed?"

"Exposed?" He furrowed his brow. "To what?"

"The Nipah." She paused, studying his features. "Isn't that what this is about? Lockdown? The epidemic?" Her stomach sank like oil droplets falling in her roommate's lava lamp. "It's something else?"

Dominic glanced at his watch. "No, the lockdown has nothing to do with Nipah. At least not directly."

"Then what is it?" She tried to keep her body from trembling, praying to God he wouldn't answer back with his usual rhetoric about confidentiality.

Another furtive glance at his watch. "Have you followed the case of the Robertson boy? The ones whose parents wanted to deny chemotherapy treatments?"

She nodded. "Yeah, I've heard a little about it."

"Well, Timothy Robertson is a patient here. His mom

brought him in two days ago. Agreed to submit to the court order. But his dad's not too happy about that. About an hour ago, he attacked the nurses who were transporting his son to radiology. Grabbed the boy and made a run for it. Got him within thirty feet of the exit to the parking garage before security stopped them. The boy's back in his room safe and sound with his mother now, but the father is still somewhere in the hospital. Apparently, he's got a history of mental instability and could be quite dangerous."

"You mean like he's armed or something?"

"I wish it were that simple." Dominic shook his head slowly.

"Then what kind of danger do you mean?"

"I mean that as we speak, the bomb squad members of the SWAT team are sweeping the ER for explosives."

"What?"

"They found evidence in Brian Robertson's house that he's been making bombs. They also found detailed blueprints of the ER."

Kennedy hadn't realized until now how small the room felt. Small and suffocating. Where did all the oxygen go? "So why don't they just evacuate?"

"This information doesn't leave the room, but one of the patients brought into the ER today has what's almost definitely a case of Nipah. Once we get this bomb thing under control, we need to know exactly who got exposed and for how long so we can keep a finger on it all."

"Wait, have you seen Carl? Is that what he's doing here?"

Dominic shook his head sadly. He looked so tired. "I don't know. I didn't have time to check on him before everything else exploded. I mean …" He cleared his throat. "Well, you know what I mean." His pager beeped, and he frowned at the screen. "I hate to do this to you, but I need to hit the ground running again. There's going to be some very scared people in the ER, and I've got to be there for them. I just couldn't stand the thought of you being in harm's way."

"What about my friends?"

He frowned. "I told them to find you and Willow and bring you both back here, but the message must have gotten garbled. We're going to do everything we can. Right now, we don't know if there's a genuine threat or not. I just want you to stay here and wait to hear from me, all right?"

Kennedy nodded. "My phone's dead."

Dominic's eyes softened but he didn't smile. "If you had a dollar for every time you let your battery die …"

Kennedy was in no mood for teasing, no matter how well intentioned. "Be safe, ok?"

"I will." He stood up and then stopped. "You be careful too." He leaned down and let his lips brush against her forehead. It was the first time he'd ever kissed her. Kennedy just wished they weren't in the middle of a hospital lockdown with a bomb scare and Nipah oubreak so that she could enjoy the moment.

"I'll be back soon, Lord-willing."

Kennedy didn't like the ominous heaviness behind his words. She forced a smile.

"Be careful," she called after him, but he was already out the door.

CHAPTER 15

Kennedy sank back in the couch, breathless and light-headed. At least she wasn't hyperventilating. Not yet.

Here she was, far enough removed from the ER so Dominic wasn't worried about a bomb blast reaching her, but how was that supposed to bring her any comfort? Everyone she cared about, every single one of her friends, was in that emergency room. The Lindgrens. Willow and Nick. And now Dominic. She squeezed her eyes shut. What she wouldn't give for a phone charger. Call her dad. Let him know what was happening.

Timothy Robertson. Kennedy hadn't followed the boy's case very thoroughly. Mostly, she'd heard details from others. Carl decrying the government overreach in depriving a couple of their parental rights. Willow was sympathetic from her homeopathic, anti-vaxxer philosophy on medicine, but the media was talking about the family as if they were negligent idiots at best and mentally unsound nutcases at worst. What was the truth? And how in the world could

Kennedy expect to get to the bottom of any of it?

She couldn't. That wasn't her job anyway. Her job was to wait here for Dominic. Pray that her friends would be ok, that they wouldn't die in some explosion or contract the Nipah virus while sitting it out in a waiting room full of potential carriers.

Her mind raced over what Dominic told her about a patient brought in earlier that day with Nipah symptoms. What if that was Carl? He couldn't die. He was so healthy. So vigorous. He had children. Grandchildren. A God-ordained ministry. He couldn't just catch some stupid disease and leave all that behind. What about his family? What would they do without him? Even worse, what if Sandy and Woong were exposed now too? What if they all ...

No. She couldn't let her mind dwell on all those horrific possibilities. Seize her thoughts. Take them captive. That's what she had to do.

Her conversation with Willow earlier about God watching over the birds got an old hymn stuck in her head. *His eye is on the sparrow.* She couldn't remember the last time she'd heard it sung in church. In fact, the only reason she knew the words was because it was on the soundtrack of one of the *Sister Act* movies. She tried to let the lyrics lead her into a spirit of worship.

She'd been working on her prayer life all semester, practicing the mental focus that was so hard to maintain in the midst of a busy, chaotic college schedule. She and Sandy talked about it quite a bit, and Sandy had been sharing some prayer tips with her, ways to keep her mind from getting distracted while she prayed. Keeping a journal was probably the most helpful thing Kennedy started. She didn't always write out her prayers verbatim. Sometimes she just jotted down short lists, but even then she found the act of putting pen to paper kept her mind far more focused than it was whenever she sat down without any plan and simply tried to talk to God.

Unfortunately, she didn't have her journal here. And her brain was far too scattered, far too anxious to allow for that quiet communion with the Lord that she'd been trying to achieve in her regular prayer times.

She stood up, hoping that pacing might help channel her focus just a little bit. Sandy sometimes prayed out loud, but even though Kennedy figured it might help keep her thoughts from wandering, she couldn't get over her crippling self-consciousness to try it. Instead, she made a compromise and started mouthing the words to what she hoped would be an effective prayer for her friends in the emergency room.

The difficult part was knowing what to pray for. Most of her energy was spent begging God to get them all out of there alive. Kennedy couldn't wait to leave the hospital. Hopefully, she wouldn't be coming back for a very long time. Maybe not until she was ready to start her residency. She'd had enough drama for the immediate future. She sighed, wondering if hospitals would always bring this sense of heaviness or if she'd get used to it once she started working in one. There were other places for doctors to put their skills to use after graduating med school. She sometimes thought about medical missions, about all the developing countries and the physicians who traveled the world serving others. Of course, she'd have to pay off her med school bills somehow, and volunteering her time while she trotted across the globe probably wasn't the best way to work off student debt. She had time to figure out all those details later, but ...

Kennedy stopped herself. Wasn't she supposed to be praying? No wonder she was such a failure in her spiritual life. She couldn't even hold a five-minute conversation with the Lord.

She sighed, remembering Sandy's admonition to be gentle with herself. *Sometimes those distractions are what God's telling us to pray about most.* But Kennedy couldn't believe that God would expect her to pray about student loans she hadn't even started to accumulate while her best friend, her boyfriend, and her pastor's family were all in danger of getting blown to pieces.

She'd just have to try again.

"Dear God." She whispered the words this time, hoping that hearing her words spoken would keep her from getting off track again. "I pray that you watch over ..."

She stopped. Was that someone coughing? Her eyes shot around the room and landed on a skinny closet. It didn't look large enough to hold more than a broom. Was she just making things up?

"Dear God," she tried again, but this time her voice was so quiet she couldn't even hear herself. "I pray that you'd watch over me while ..."

Another cough. Kennedy froze halfway between the closet and the exit, her mind too stunned to react. Her body stood frozen, ready to protect herself or ready to run away but unable to decide which she would need to do first.

She braced herself in the ready stance she'd learned in her self-defense class as the closet door swung open. Her eyes focused on the barrel of a gun before they made out the features of the man holding it.

"Hands up," he ordered. His voice was nearly as quiet as hers had been while she was trying to pray. He waved the gun in her direction. "Step away from that door. Slow and easy."

Kennedy had no choice but to obey.

CHAPTER 16

"I don't want to hurt you. Got that? The last thing I want to do is hurt you." He took a step closer to Kennedy.

She hurried behind the couch. Anywhere to put more distance, more obstacles between herself and her intruder.

He locked the deadbolt of the conference room. "Listen, you don't have to be afraid." He slid a small loveseat in front of the door as a barricade. "I'm not planning to hurt anyone."

He sounded so earnest. Like he was scared of himself. So why did he have a gun?

"What's your name?" He nodded at the couch. "You can sit down. We're going to be here a while, I'm guessing. May as well get comfortable."

Finding a cozy seat was the last thing on Kennedy's mind.

"Who are you?" he asked. "What are you doing here?"

She ran through all of her dad's stupid crisis training lectures. Had any of them prepared her for this?

"My name's Kennedy Stern. I'm a college student at Harvard." There. Give him details to prove that she was a flesh-and-blood human. Not some sacrifice or human shield he could hide behind.

"Harvard, eh?" He raised his eyebrows. "Impressive. What're you studying?"

"Biology." She couldn't raise her eyes to his. Hated the thought of that gun in his hand. Couldn't find anywhere to focus her gaze. Wasn't she supposed to be praying?

"Oh, yeah? Premed?" She nodded, and he let out a little scoff. "Be a doctor, save the world? Is that the goal?"

She didn't reply.

"Let me guess. You're really smart, but you've got something of a bleeding-heart complex, so you're going into medicine to improve the lives of your patients. Did I get that about right?"

She glanced at the locked door. Someone would find her. Dominic would come to check on her. All she had to do was stay calm. Stay focused.

His eye is on the sparrow, and I know he watches me …

The man shrugged. "I guess you're young enough not to know any better." He sat down on the opposite side of the couch, keeping a full cushion length between them. "Doctors. Thinking you can play God. Thinking you alone possess the power to choose who's going to be healed and who isn't."

He lifted his eyes to hers and held her gaze. "Do you know who I am?"

She had a good suspicion but still hadn't found her voice.

"I'm Brian Robertson. My son Timothy, you've heard about him in the news maybe."

She nodded slightly.

"I don't want to hurt anybody." His voice sounded reassuring, but he still hadn't let go of his weapon. "I swear, I don't want to hurt you." There was something earnest in his voice. Something that made Kennedy feel like he needed to convince her. He shook his head. "I'm so sorry. You must be terrified." He slid his gun into the holster and reached for a bottle of water from the coffee table. "Need a drink? Go on. Take it. It's perfectly safe. I haven't even opened it."

Kennedy reached out. Hoped he didn't see the way her whole body trembled.

"Drink it," he ordered again. "You'll feel better. Man, I must have really terrified you. I hope you'll forgive me."

Kennedy took a few small sips from the bottle, felt the cool water slip down her throat.

"That better?" he asked.

"A little."

"Good. See? I'm trying to help. Just like you becoming a doctor. You and me both, we're just trying to heal people. Know what I mean? It's just that only one of us is doing it God's way."

Kennedy stared. Wondered how long it would take before Dominic realized she was trapped in here. He was a man of prayer. A man full of the Holy Spirit. Couldn't God tell him she was in trouble? Tell him to come back to the conference room and check on her? Dominic was the kind of believer who would listen to that sort of thing. Follow those promptings, those Holy Spirit urges.

Please, God. Tell him to come back.

"So you know why I'm here?" Brian leaned back in his seat and stretched his arm across the back of the couch.

"I'm guessing it has something to do with your son."

He nodded. "My wife and me, we love that kid to death. Didn't get pregnant until I was forty-one. Shannon, she was thirty-eight. We'd tried everything by then. Almost given up. Turns out all we needed to do was stop doubting and believe. Believe that God would give us the child he promised. And he did. When our little Timmy came to us — you've never met a better baby. I swear, you've never met a better little boy." He stared past Kennedy's shoulder. "Do you remember your first day of grade school?"

"Not that well."

"Know what our Timmy was doing the first day of school? Having his third MRI. Know where he lost his first tooth? Right here at Providence. Peds floor. Know where he spent his sixth birthday? The hospital cafeteria. His aunt and cousin came and we ate plain rice with raisins before wheeling him back up to the oncology ward of the Children's Hospital. Think that's the kind of life any little boy deserves?"

Kennedy shook her head. If she kept on agreeing with Brian, if she kept him from getting upset, this whole scenario might end peacefully.

He frowned. "Not the kind of life he deserves at all. Which is why last summer, Shannon and I took him to a Cameron Hopewell crusade. You know him? Gift of healing. He's the one who told us God would cure our son, but he wanted to do it without the aid of Western medicine. That's the only way God would get all the glory. So we told the oncologist we were done. Done with the tests, done with the chemo, done with the poison they were drip-feeding him through those IVs. We believed God was going to heal our son, and he was going to do it through natural remedies and the power of prayer." He let out a mirthless laugh. "Three hundred thousand dollars in lawyer fees later, and you know what? Here we are. Right back where we started."

"That's got to be really hard."

"Know what Timmy told Shannon he wished for last Christmas? He told her he wished God would come down and carry him off to heaven so he wouldn't have to hurt anymore."

Kennedy bit her lip.

"What kind of monsters do this to a family? Do this to a child? Bishop Hopewell didn't say alternative medicine was out. He just said no more radiation. No more chemotherapy. It's not like we've been negligent. We took Timmy to several clinics, plunked down fifty grand for one consultation with the country's most renowned naturopath. We had another virtual consult set up with an herbal oncology expert in Switzerland. He's cured over a dozen cases just like Timmy's. I don't see all those other parents getting lined up and fined. I don't see judges threatening to remove their children from their homes, land them in state custody." He let out a heavy sigh. "You ever know anyone with cancer?"

"Yeah, my grandma."

"She die of it?"

"Uh-huh." She stared at a painting behind Brian's shoulder. The portrait was of some stuffy-looking businessman, maybe one of the hospital's founders or patrons.

"Did your grandma get chemo? Radiation?"

Kennedy nodded.

"And still died, huh?"

Another nod.

Brian lowered his head. "I'm sorry to hear that."

"I'm sorry for your son, too," Kennedy whispered.

"You must think I'm a horrible person."

She searched his face, hunting for clues that he was trying to trap her. She only saw pained earnestness. "No, I don't think that." She knew what was happening. Brian was trying to prey on her feelings of helplessness. Trying to convince her that he was doing the right thing. It was a classic case of Stockholm syndrome. Cognitive dissonance morphing into misplaced sympathies.

"Well, you have kids one day, maybe you'll understand. Heaven forbid they have to go through what my little Timmy has."

Kennedy didn't know how to respond.

"It just doesn't make sense. You've got heroin addicts, prostitutes, abusive drunks — they all get to keep their kids. Abused children falling through the cracks in the system because someone passes one drug screen or takes one two-hour anger management seminar. But we're the negligent ones. We're the ones who would lose custody of our kid unless we bring him here, strap him to a gurney, listen to him scream his little heart out while nurses poke and prod his veins. It's a test. I kept telling my wife God was going to test us, but she couldn't stand the thought of Timmy being taken away from us, no matter what Bishop Hopewell said. In the court's mind, we're the bad parents. We're the ones who don't know what's best for our child. We're the religious nutcases who would rather see our son cured by the Holy Spirit, who heals completely and fully and doesn't leave horrific side effects. But we're told that we have to accept their poison, that if we don't consent to chemo and radiation, not only will our son die, but he'll die in the custody of foster parents while we rot in jail for neglect."

Kennedy's plan of placating Brian wasn't working. She had to calm him down. "I remember my grandma wondering if it was worth going through another round of treatments." Her voice was shaky, but she ignored the fear in her gut. "By that point, the doctors said it wouldn't do much other than buy her a few more months. But she was so uncomfortable the whole time. I think she did it for her kids though. They wanted her to hold on a little longer."

Brian nodded. "That's pretty common. That's because doctors can't heal. No offense to you, but you may as well accept it right now. Doctors don't cure. They treat a few symptoms, rack up the big bucks, and that's it. You believe in God?" he asked.

She nodded, thankful to see his shoulders relax slightly even though she wasn't equipped to jump into the middle of a theological debate. That was a calling for someone like Dominic, someone who'd studied up on the issues and had all the right answers to offer. She was ready to change the subject when Brian asked, "What religion are you?"

"Oh." She felt her face heat up and hated herself for it. Didn't the Bible tell her to be ready at any moment to explain her faith to those who asked? Of course, she'd never expected to be asked by someone who'd been pointing a gun at her face just a few minutes earlier. "I'm a Christian." She tried to slow down her breathing. Why did that make her so nervous to admit?

He nodded. "Born again, Bible believing, all that stuff?"

She nodded. "I guess so."

"So you know exactly what I'm talking about. How our Savior healed people by faith. How faith — believing the Holy Spirit dwells inside you — can cure even the most fatal diseases. That's what we've been trying to teach Timmy. He's young, of course, but sometimes it's that childlike faith that makes the difference. You know what I mean? Jesus talks about it all the time. The faith of a child, it's strong enough to move mountains."

Kennedy wasn't sure he was quoting the passage right, but she didn't have it memorized and wouldn't have had the guts to correct him even if she did.

Brian's voice was animated. "The Bible talks about it all over the place. *Call on the elders, and the prayers offered up in faith will raise the sick to life.*"

Another reference Kennedy wasn't sure if he was botching or not. It sounded slightly familiar, but she wouldn't have even known where to look it up in the Bible if she had one with her.

"That's what it is my wife and I were trying to get that judge to understand. It's not only the fact that these treatments are harmful to our son. It's that it undermines whatever faith we're hoping to instill in him. We took him to meet Cameron Hopewell at two different crusades. The bishop told us Timmy would be cured, but we couldn't go back to the oncologists. That's what he said. God wanted to cure our son, but he wanted to be the one who got the glory for it. And by bringing him back here, by accepting the drugs and radiation and all that, it's like spitting in God's face after the healing he promised us."

Kennedy was lost on a theological level, but at least

Brian sounded sincere. Or was that the cognitive dissonance playing tricks with her head? The Stockholm syndrome. Making her believe he was sympathetic since being trapped with a loving, wise father who just wanted what was best for his child was easier to accept than being trapped with a desperate, armed father who was also a raving lunatic.

In the end, it didn't matter what Kennedy thought of Brian or his son Timothy or the family court's order to submit to chemotherapy or relinquish parental rights.

It didn't matter because in the end, it was still Brian who had that gun, and Kennedy was sitting beside him, praying to God and hoping to heaven that he wouldn't decide to use it.

CHAPTER 17

"You ever watch faith healers on TV?" Brian asked after a few moments.

The question startled her. "Faith healers?"

"You know, Bishop Hopewell, others like him. Praying for the sick, curing them right there in front of thousands of witnesses."

"No. I've never watched them do that."

"They get a bad rap because they charge money for their events. As if any other Christian minister doesn't have the right to earn their living by their work. I don't see them complaining about Christian authors charging a fair price for their books, do you? Or pastors asking their congregations for a monthly paycheck. But Cameron Hopewell charges a hundred dollars for one of his healing handkerchiefs that he's personally prayed over, and people throw a fit. Say he's a charlatan. You know why he charges that much money, don't you?"

Kennedy figured greed and gullibility had quite a bit to do with it, but Brian was ready with an answer of his own.

"Faith. Just like Jesus turned out the crowds who didn't have enough faith to see Jairus's daughter raised up to life. The only people he wanted around were the people he knew actually expected the miracle to happen. So you ask someone to believe that God will use a healing handkerchief to cure their disease, and if they're willing to pay that hundred dollars, it shows they have enough faith for that healing to work. You go around sending free handkerchiefs to everybody, you get all the folks who don't have enough faith, so of course they aren't going to get the same results. Not to mention you go bankrupt and can't continue on in your work for the Lord.

"It's scientific fact. You can appreciate that. That's why patients receiving a placebo still show signs of improvement. Because they believe the medicine's going to help them, and that faith is what brings them healing. They've done experiments on it, you know. If the patient has to pay for a placebo, or even if they're simply told that the drug is expensive, there's a higher chance of recovery. Just from a sugar pill. It's not wacky science. It's faith, pure and simple. You have faith, you find your healing. Just like Jesus talks about in the New Testament."

Kennedy didn't know what to say. She'd read some of those same studies about placebos, but she'd never thought about it in the context of Christian faith or miraculous healings.

"You think I'm crazy, don't you?" Brian asked.

Kennedy forced herself to shake her head. Reminded herself that in this situation it was perfectly acceptable to lie to keep herself out of danger. "You're not crazy. You're just a father trying to look out for his son."

He sighed. "I never expected it to come to this. Look at me. A year ago, I was bringing in three hundred grand a year. Three hundred stinking grand. Does that sound like the kind of father who would lose his son to state custody? Does that sound like the kind of father who would bring a gun into a crowded hospital, who would risk ..." His voice caught.

Kennedy tried to steer the conversation away from his schemes. She tried to think of something to say. Anything that would get Brian's mind off of his gun or any other plans he'd made. "How is your son doing right now? I mean, how is his health?"

Brian let out his breath in a controlled hiss. "They started the chemo yesterday. He's been puking all morning and is too sick to eat. Doctors are talking about surgery to put in a feeding tube right into his intestine. Bypass the stomach entirely."

"I'm sorry. What's your wife think of all this?"

"Shannon? She tried to be strong, but the devil knew where she was weakest and attacked her the hardest. She idolizes that child. Couldn't think of the state taking him away, even when I told her this was all just a test from God. A test I just hope I'm strong enough to pass ..."

Kennedy realized the conversation was still veering too close to Brian and whatever plans he'd conceived to rescue his child. But what else could she talk about? It's not like she could strike up a conversation about the weather.

Brian scowled at the floor for several seconds. Kennedy glanced surreptitiously at his wristwatch, but she didn't know what time it had been when Dominic left her here. Didn't know how long they'd already been waiting.

"You got Internet on your phone?" he asked. "I wonder if the news has already picked up the story."

"No, my batteries are dead."

"Just as well. Otherwise, you'd probably have found a way to call the cops on me by now, right?"

Kennedy still wanted to keep him placated. "I wouldn't do that."

"Oh, yes you would. Don't be afraid to admit it. I'm not saying I'm doing the right thing here. But what choice do I have? God told me through the bishop that the only way my son would be cured was if we deny the chemotherapy. It's a hard road, but it's the one he's called me to walk. And my son's worth it."

Kennedy didn't want to hear any more excuses. She glanced at the screen on the wall. "There's a TV over there. Maybe you could watch the news on that." She tried to keep her voice steady while she planned how fast she'd have to act to move the loveseat, unlock the door, and escape while he fiddled with the television controls. She was pretty sure after talking to him that he wouldn't shoot her in the back while she ran.

But what if she was wrong?

Brian tilted his head toward the small shelf. "Go over there and hand me that remote."

So much for attempting to flee. For a second, Kennedy thought about simply asking him to let her leave. Promising she wouldn't tell the guards where he was if he just unlocked that door. Instead, she walked slowly over to the far wall, keenly aware of his eyes on her. She handed him the remote.

"Thank you." So polite. So gallant.

"You're welcome." She couldn't make herself speak in anything more than a whisper.

"Please don't think I'm a monster." His voice was so earnest. Kennedy forced herself to look straight at him.

"No," she lied. "I don't think that at all."

CHAPTER 18

Providence Hospital was the first image that popped onto the television screen. A news anchor stood out front of the entrance, and the camera panned wide to get a shot of all the police cars stationed outside.

"I'm here in front of Providence Hospital, where the general director has issued a hospital-wide lockdown. At this point, it's only speculation what the problem is or whether or not it has anything to do with the Nipah scare that's now blown to full pandemic proportions. With New York in a state of emergency and Florida expected to follow suit, it's anyone's guess right now whether Massachusetts will be the next state to shut its borders in hopes of stopping the spread of the disease. Meanwhile, in Medford ..."

Brian shut off the volume and swore.

"Not what you wanted to hear?" Kennedy asked.

"It just makes me so sick. Here we are in the middle of a pandemic, and my son's dragged out of his home where we could have kept him isolated, free from exposure, and instead he's brought here. I swear, if he doesn't die from the chemo, it'll be the Nipah next, and his precious soul is going to be on the consciences of all the lawyers and all the attorneys and all the stinking politicians in this whole mess of a country. God will hold them accountable, I tell you that much."

"It's not going to come to that." Kennedy forced conviction into her voice even though all she could focus on was escape. Out of all the rooms Dominic could have led her to, he picked the hiding spot of a murderous father.

No, not murderous. He hadn't hurt anybody yet. And hadn't he promised her several times, assured her he didn't want to harm her? Was that the truth or was that just what he told Kennedy to keep her in line?

Brian shook his head. "I just wish …"

Kennedy's breath caught in her throat. "Wait," she interrupted. "Wait. Turn the volume back up." She stared at the familiar face on the television screen while Diane Fiddlestein, one of Channel 2's studio reporters, talked into the camera. "Turn it up," she told him again and reached out for the remote.

"I got it," he said and unmuted the TV.

"… admitted to the ER with a fever and swelling of the brain."

Kennedy's lungs were paralyzed. Brian could have pulled out his gun and held it to her temple right then and she couldn't have been more surprised.

"The patient's symptoms came on suddenly this afternoon, and he is currently being treated in an isolation room at Providence."

"Do you know him?" Brian asked.

"Shh."

"The patient's family has included this photograph so that anyone who's come into contact can take necessary precautions."

Kennedy leaned forward as if that would keep her from missing any of the words. "Turn it up."

"Doctors have sent lab samples to the CDC. They can't confirm Nipah at this stage, however they are recommending that anyone who's had exposure to the patient in the past two days monitor their temperature every hour, avoid crowded areas, and seek medical attention immediately if symptoms appear."

Kennedy probably hadn't blinked during the entire segment. They still hadn't taken the picture off the screen. It couldn't be. It wasn't possible. He'd been perfectly healthy ...

"Who is that?"

Kennedy couldn't answer. She shook her head, disbelief coursing through her system. He'd said something about a headache, but that didn't mean ...

"Who is that kid?" Brian asked again.

The news anchor continued her report, even though Kennedy's brain did its best to shut out every word.

She lowered her head. "His name is Woong."

CHAPTER 19

Breathe. She couldn't breathe. Her counselor had given her an assignment. There was something she was supposed to do when she felt the start of a panic attack. She was supposed to look around. Find… Find what? What was there to find while she was stuck in a cramped conference room with a deranged father who was ready to blow the brains out of anyone who got between him and his son? What was there to listen for when all she could hear was the droning on of Diane Fiddlestein's nasally voice as she talked about Woong Lindgren as if he was some nameless patient and not the spunky, mischievous little boy Kennedy had been watching for the past two days?

Woong. Too curious for his own good, asking more questions than Tom Cruise in *A Few Good Men*, but sweet enough to work his way into the hardest of hearts.

Woong. He couldn't be sick. Kennedy tried to remember what time it'd been when they first arrived at the hospital. He'd been fine. Complained a little bit about his legs aching in the morning, and that was all. That and a little headache. Otherwise, he was totally normal. He wasn't sick. He couldn't be sick.

Brian swore and turned off the TV. "Nothing. Not a single word about my son."

Kennedy wasn't sure what he'd expected.

"If it weren't for that outbreak ..."

Someone knocked on the door. "Kennedy?"

Air rushed back into her lungs. She glutted herself on the influx of oxygen.

"Kennedy?"

"Who's that?" Brian stared at the barricaded door and then at her. "You know that guy? Who is he?"

"It's the chaplain," she told him.

"The one you were talking to earlier?"

She nodded.

"Kennedy! It's me. You can unlock the door. Kennedy?"

Brian grabbed her by the upper arm, his fingers pinching into her flesh. "Not a word," he snarled in her ear. "Got that? Not a cough, not a hiccup, don't even think of breathing loud."

"Kennedy!"

Brian jerked her by the arm off the couch. "Come on."

She didn't ask where he was taking her. Didn't dare make a noise. She tripped over one of her stupid sandals as he yanked her toward the broom closet. Dumb heels. She kicked them off. She had to be ready to run when she got the chance.

"Kennedy!" Dominic's voice was strained. Tense. Did he have any idea what was happening? Had he put enough of the pieces together to figure out what was going on?

Brian shoved Kennedy into the closet while Dominic jostled the doorknob. Brian pulled out his gun. *No!* She had to warn Dominic about the weapon. But how can you scream when you don't have any breath? How can you warn your boyfriend away from imminent danger when you can't even control your own lungs?

Brian hefted her up. She was in his arms now, her bare feet dangling a foot off the ground. "Get up there," he grumbled. Kennedy reached up into an open air vent. Did he expect her to crawl through? "Get up," he repeated and pushed her higher, his hands on the back pockets of her pants as he tried to force her through the narrow opening.

Now she wished she'd kept her sandals on. "No!" she screamed and kicked. She'd been aiming for his nose but ended up with her heel smashing into his eye socket instead. She gave him one more sturdy kick to knock him off his balance and jumped down. Pain raced up both ankles when she landed.

He grabbed her by the wrist as she tried to run past him. She kicked his shin without causing any harm. Why hadn't she thought to bring better shoes? She'd trade in her GPA for a pair of spiked cleats right about now.

He had both arms wrapped around her, and she felt something hard across his chest. A bullet-proof vest, maybe? She'd have to warn Dominic and the security officers when they got into the room.

"Stop struggling, will you?" His breath was hot against her ear. She flailed in his grip, fighting to be set free but causing about as much damage as Simba the lion cub wrestling with his dad.

She snapped her head back. Controlled, forceful, like she'd practiced so many times in her self-defense class. She heard the snap of cartilage, Brian's angry curse as he bent over. It was the chance she needed. With a grunt of exertion, she freed herself from his hold and ran to the door. She flung back the deadbolt as she strained to push the barricade aside. "Dominic!" she shouted. "He's got a gun! Be careful!"

The door opened a few inches before hitting the loveseat. Kennedy was stuck between the couch and the wall.

"Kennedy!" Dominic's voice flooded her senses with relief. It was ok. Everything was going to be ok.

Brian grabbed Kennedy by the collar of her shirt. The

cold metal of his pistol pressed hard against her temple. "Don't move," he told Dominic. "I've got a gun to her head. You step inside, I shoot."

"It's ok." Dominic's voice was reassuring. Calm.

The door was open, but only slightly. Kennedy couldn't see Dominic on the other side. She was afraid the second he poked his head around the corner, Brian would turn the gun on him and shoot. Her body was too terrified to even tremble.

"Listen, Brian. My name's Dominic. Dominic Martinez. I'm a chaplain. I'm not here to arrest you. I'm not here to get you into any sort of trouble. I just want to talk, maybe pray with you. You're a man of prayer, aren't you?"

Kennedy held her breath. If anyone could talk down a psycho with a loaded gun aimed at her occipital lobe, Dominic was the man for the job.

Brian didn't respond.

After a minute, Dominic continued. "Listen, we know about the explosives. We know you had hospital blueprints in your home. If you help me out, you can keep a lot of people from getting hurt. Good people, Brian. Can you help me?"

"Why would I do that?" he snarled.

Kennedy didn't know if it was wishful thinking or not,

but she thought she sensed him lessen his grip. If the stupid loveseat wasn't in the way, she could run. As it was, she was pinned between the partially-opened door and the wall. Was this how she was going to die, with Dominic there on the other side, so close, so helpless?

"You're a good man, Brian. Lots of people know that. A man of faith. Everything you're doing, you're doing because you think it's best for your son. And now I'm asking you to think about the other people, too. There's a lot of scared folks in the ER, Brian. Some of them are kids. Same age as your little guy. I know you want them to be able to go home and spend a safe, peaceful night with their families, right? So I need you to tell me where the bomb is. If you help me, then all these innocent people don't have to get hurt."

"You think the bomb's in the ER?" he asked. His voice had lost its hardened edge. Were Dominic's calm presence and softly spoken words actually working?

"We found the blueprints of yours. But our teams have looked everywhere and we haven't found it yet. So we're hoping you can go ahead and tell us. It'd mean a lot to those scared boys and girls who just want to be safe."

"There's no bomb in the ER."

Kennedy couldn't be sure, but it sounded like a boast.

"We know you were building something, Brian. Can you

tell us what you were planning? I want to help you and your family. I really do. I'm not saying what that judge did was right. But if you go on like this, if you injure a bunch of innocent people, there's no chance the legal system's going to change its mind. You know that, right?"

"Maybe."

It wasn't happening. It couldn't be happening. Kennedy didn't dare raise her hopes too high. Was Dominic actually about to convince Brian to give up the location of the explosive?

"So where's the bomb, Brian? We really want to take care of this so all these scared people can go home and be safe."

"It's not in the ER," he repeated.

"Then where?"

Brian loosened his hold. This time, Kennedy was sure of it.

"Brian?" Dominic's voice revealed a strain of tension. "Talk to me, buddy. What's going on behind that door?"

"Why don't you come in here and find out?" The words themselves might have sounded ominous, but Brian's tone was polite and subdued.

Kennedy mentally begged Dominic not to listen. The minute he exposed himself, Brian could shoot.

"Ok, I'm stepping into the conference room right now, all right?"

Kennedy squinted, preparing to close her eyes so she wouldn't have to watch her boyfriend getting murdered.

"I'm keeping my hands up. I don't have a gun or anything, ok? I'm nothing but the chaplain. Just here to talk. That's all I want to do."

Kennedy's legs nearly collapsed when Dominic walked slowly into the room and stood in front of them. His eyes flickered once to her then settled back on Brian.

"Now listen to me. I've already said I don't want to hurt you. I'm just here to get a little information, ok?"

Brian didn't answer.

"I want us to trust each other, Brian. And right now, it's hard for us to trust each other when you have that gun to an innocent girl's head. See what I'm saying? What if you set it down for a minute? I don't mean to take it from you. That's not what I'm suggesting. I just think we all might be a little more comfortable if you put it back in its holster. What do you say about that?"

"I think I'll wait and see for myself and make sure you don't have an army of SWAT team members behind you for backup."

"That's ok with me. I can understand a smart guy like

you wanting to be as cautious as possible. But tell me something. My friend you've got there, her name's Kennedy. And I know you and I both would hate to see anything bad accidentally happen to her. So maybe what you can do is let her go, and then you and I can keep up our conversation."

Brian didn't say anything, and he didn't let go either. Kennedy stared at the clock. She had never experienced such long seconds in her life.

Brian let out his breath. Kennedy thought she felt his body tremble just a little.

Come on, Dominic. Keep him calm. No matter what it takes, you've got to keep him calm.

"By the way, I've got a message from your wife," Dominic said. "From Shannon. She wants you to know Timmy's doing well. She said the side effects haven't been too bad this round. There's a chance I could ask and see if we could get you to talk to her on the phone. Would you like that? To talk to your wife?"

"What do you want from me?" Brian shifted his weight from one foot to the other.

"What I want is to know what you've done with the explosives you made. Is that something you think we can talk about now?"

Kennedy felt Brian nod. The motion was so slight she was afraid at first she imagined it, but Dominic must have seen it too.

"Good. Because the sooner you tell us about the explosives, the sooner this whole thing is over for all of us. What did you do with the bomb, Brian? Where did you put it?"

Now Kennedy was sure Brian was trembling.

"I'll tell you, but first the girl gets behind me."

"Listen," Dominic said, glancing once again at Kennedy. She couldn't read his expression. "I'm really grateful you're ready to talk about that bomb. Really grateful. But I want you to think about Kennedy for a minute. She's been through a lot. She's scared …"

"I'll do it," Kennedy interrupted. She was surprised at the forcefulness of her own voice. "I'll do it," she repeated. As long as Brian holstered that gun. As long as he remained calm. As long as he told Dominic where the bomb was, she didn't care where she stood. Without waiting to hear any arguments, she stepped several paces back. She didn't know why Brian wanted her behind him, but she was thankful to be free from his hold. She backed up until she was standing near the closet with the air vent.

"Ok," Dominic said. "I'm listening."

Kennedy was dizzy. Dizzy and weak. Her legs could hardly support her weight.

Brian started to unbutton his shirt.

"What are you doing?" Was that fear now in Dominic's voice? That voice that had remained so calm and composed for so long? "Brian?" he asked again. His words were shaky.

Brian took one arm out of his shirt sleeve and then the other. Kennedy could see it now, too. Could understand the tension in Dominic's tone.

"Here it is." Brian pointed to the heavy vest strapped to his chest, covered in wires. "This is the bomb you've been looking for."

CHAPTER 20

"Kennedy, I want you to get behind me." It was the first time Dominic had spoken directly to her since he entered the room.

Brian shook his head. "No. She shouldn't do that."

"Kennedy, do it." Dominic's voice was authoritative, no longer soothing and calm but laden with emotion. "Get behind me. Right now."

Brian aimed the gun at Dominic. "I said she shouldn't do that."

"Now listen." Dominic held out one hand in a conciliatory gesture. "She doesn't have anything to do with any of this. She's just a girl who was at the wrong place at the wrong time ..."

His words echoed mirthlessly in Kennedy's terrified mind. *Wrong place at the wrong time.* Yeah, story of her life.

Dominic was staring at her again. Addressing her directly. "He's not gonna shoot me, Kennedy. Now you come this way and get behind me."

Even from where she stood several feet away, Kennedy could feel the heat of Brian's growing anger. Dominic was wrong. He wasn't thinking clearly. All he was doing was making a crazy man strapped with explosives even more agitated.

Shut up, Dominic. She wished telepathy really worked.

"The girl stays where she is." Brian's voice trembled. Shakier than it had been throughout this entire engagement. Dominic didn't know who he was dealing with. Didn't know what this man was capable of.

"Kennedy," he barked again. "Come here and get behind me."

The hand that held Brian's gun shook violently.

Kennedy's limbs refused to move. Her ears rushed with the sound of her pounding pulse.

Dominic took a step forward. "Listen, Brian, I know you love your son. That's what makes you such a good father for him."

Kennedy wondered how he could get the words out without wincing.

"So what I want you to do right now is think about Timothy. Think about how much he needs you. This isn't about his treatment anymore. This isn't about what medicine he is or isn't going to take. This is about your son needing to know his dad is one of the good guys. How is Timothy going to feel if he grows up and learns you killed yourself and a whole bunch of innocent people? How will that make Timothy feel?"

"He won't have a chance to grow up if I don't do what I've got to do." Brian's voice trembled just as much as the gun in his hand, which was still aimed at Dominic's chest.

"Listen." Dominic's tone grew more authoritative as he spoke. "What you're about to do, it's not going to help your son at all. It's just going to take away his father. What if Timothy learns how many other people you killed, too? What will he think about you then?"

"He'll think he had a father who did what he had to do when he was faced with an impossible test."

Kennedy's lungs took in oxygen a few puny milliliters at a time.

"You and I both know that's not how he's going to see it." Dominic took a step forward. "So why don't you put that gun down ..."

"Not gonna happen."

"I really think you might want to ..." Dominic began.

"I really think you might want to shut up." Brian poised his finger on the trigger.

Kennedy braced herself, her only hope that Brian was so

distraught it would throw off his aim.

"You don't want to do this." Dominic's voice betrayed no fear. Kennedy wished he could lend her some of his confidence. He hadn't looked at her in several minutes. It was as if he were in some sort of mental zone and was deliberately ignoring her. Maybe that made it easier for him. Pretend he was in a room with a nameless victim, an anonymous bystander, not his own girlfriend.

Kennedy tried to control her breath. *Please, God, don't let him die.*

With his free hand, Brian pulled a cell phone out of his pocket. "I press one button, we all get blown to bits, got it?"

Dominic nodded. "Ok. I hear you. I understand. Don't you think you'll feel better once you give that phone to me?" He reached his hand out and took a step forward.

No! Kennedy wanted to yell the word, but she was afraid any sudden sound would startle Brian into detonating his explosive vest. She cringed. Tried to look away. Tried to brace herself for the fatal blast she knew was coming.

"Get back." Brian's voice rose in pitch. Didn't Dominic see how worked-up he was getting? How desperate?

"Ok." Dominic held up both hands. "All right. I'm sorry. I'll stand here by the door. Will that make you feel better?"

Kennedy imagined her body turning into a small ball.

Like an armadillo that could wrap itself up in its own personal, bomb-proof armor. She thought about the closet behind her. If she could get to it, somehow get up to that crawl space ...

But she couldn't leave Dominic here. Not alone. Any sudden move would spell death for them both. She still wasn't sure if Dominic was the man she was meant to spend the rest of her life with. Up until now, she'd figured she could take months or even years to figure that out. She certainly never expected them both to die together a few short months into their relationship at the hand of a deranged explosives engineer.

Brian still held the cell phone in his hand. At least while he was focused on it, he wasn't aiming the gun at Dominic's chest, but that was only a small comfort considering the fact that if he detonated that bomb, Kennedy, Dominic, and anyone unfortunate enough to be in the proximity of the explosion would die.

I didn't even get to say good-bye to my parents. Kennedy's body had stopped trembling. She leaned against the wall, unable to stand on her own. Unable to take in the horror that surrounded her. Her mind had wrapped itself up into some sort of emotional cocoon. She wasn't scared. She couldn't describe what it was she felt. Like her brain was filtering out the raw horror of the situation, only allowing tiny bits and pieces of realization to settle into her being a few seconds at a time. Even though she appreciated the mental numbness compared to the paralyzing weight of panic, she felt her body was too sluggish to know what to do if the chance came to react. Her body was maxed out on adrenaline. The fight or flight response wouldn't work. Not right now. She'd sooner pass out from weakness than find a way to save herself.

She had to get her mind more alert, but to do that, she had to admit the terror. Welcome the devastating horror that would crash through her psyche like the tsunami in *Deep Impact* if she let even the slightest trace of fear slip past her emotional barriers.

Brian's cell phone trembled in his hand. "You're both my witnesses that I'm doing this for my son."

"There are other ways, you know." Dominic took a step forward.

Brian was so concentrated on his phone he didn't seem to notice.

"Your son can have a comfortable life. You'll have other chances to show him how much you love him."

Brian shook his head. "This is my test. I can't fail."

Dominic took another step. "I know you feel helpless. I

know you feel desperate and lost. I would too. But blowing yourself up, that's only going to create a lot more problems for your family, don't you think?"

"I don't care." He holstered his gun. Five minutes ago, the gesture would have brought a flood of relief crashing through Kennedy's system. Now she realized how tame a single pistol looked compared to a homemade explosive vest.

How far would the blast radius extend? How many people would die? How many more would be injured?

How would the authorities tell her parents about Kennedy's death?

She'd never gotten the chance to introduce them to her boyfriend.

A hollow chasm radiated out from the pit of her gut, ripping that emotional armor she'd erected into tiny shreds. She didn't want to die. Didn't want her last vision on earth to be Dominic's calm face right before the two of them were blown apart by the force of a violent explosion.

How did a detonation kill you exactly? Was it all the shrapnel slicing through your body's vital organs? Or was it the energy itself? Would it be hot? Would she feel it at all? Would she even know she was about to die? Or would she simply blink and find herself in heaven? It was too late to wonder now. She'd find out soon enough. She'd expected so much more out of her life. Out of her relationship with Dominic.

He'd never kissed her yet, at least not for real.

She wasn't ready to go.

What about Willow? Her roommate was so new to the faith. Had so much growing to do. Kennedy wanted to be there for that. To witness God finish what he'd started in her.

Dominic's voice was tense but it didn't quiver. "Listen to me, Brian. You're going to feel a whole lot better when you give me that phone, all right?"

"You want the phone, do you?" Brian's tone was deathly calm.

No! Kennedy's whole spirit screamed out as Brian's fingers tensed around his cell.

"Kennedy, get down!"

Dominic's panicked cry was drowned out by the horrific eruption that burst in her ears and the terror that exploded all around her.

CHAPTER 21

Beep. Beep. Beep.

Was she dead?

"Vitals stabilizing."

"Pressure starting to rise."

Beep. Beep. Beep.

Where was she?

"Let's get her transferred."

"Careful."

Her body swinging. Pain in her arm. She tried to speak but couldn't.

Beep. Beep. Beep.

"Kennedy? Is your name Kennedy Stern? Can you hear me?"

Why couldn't she form any words?

"You're going to be ok. We're taking good care of you."

Thank you, she tried to mouth. She was heavy. Her whole body was heavy. Her ears echoed with the screeches of terror. Was she even conscious?

She couldn't remember where she was. All she knew was she didn't want to be here.

God, I want to go home.

A desperate prayer. Did he hear her? Did he see her? Was she all alone?

Beep.

Beep.

Beep.

CHAPTER 22

Kennedy blinked herself awake. How long had she been knocked out? Her eyes were dry, as if her contacts had crusted onto her corneas.

Thirsty. She was thirsty.

"Easy, now." The voice was garbled somehow, like someone talking at her through a wall of water. An enormous hand covered with a yellow glove held her down.

She tried to ask for a drink, but all that came out was, *Wifter.*

"Calm down. You were injured, but you're going to be just fine."

Kennedy's eyes traveled up from the hands to the giant rubber suit. The hazmat helmet.

"Where am I?" This time, the words came out more clearly.

"You're in an isolation unit."

She blinked as memories coursed and flooded through her brain.

The explosion. The lockdown. The epidemic.

"Am I sick?"

She didn't know if the healthcare worker was avoiding her gaze or if the helmet just distorted the view.

"Am I sick?" she repeated, assessing her beaten, battered body. Her arm throbbed. She couldn't turn her head without experiencing a horrific muscle spasm throughout her entire neck. The entire right half of her body felt so heavy she was sure it must be swollen to twice its usual size. A piercing headache. Her heart fluttering slightly and her lungs still stinging from the aftershocks of terror and smoke. Bruises on her hip. An excruciating pain radiating outward from her tailbone. At least she didn't feel feverish. That must be a good sign.

"No, you're not sick. This is just a precaution. You were potentially exposed before the accident," the nurse explained. "We're treating your injuries in isolation just to be safe."

It took Kennedy a few seconds to piece everything together, to remember why she'd ended up at the hospital in the first place. The epidemic. The man with the gun. The news reports. "Is Woong ok?"

"The little boy you were babysitting? We're keeping him under quarantine until we get the lab results back. He's got the right symptoms for Nipah, but it will be another day until we know for sure. The good news is if you remain symptom-free, you can be released from isolation tomorrow evening."

Tomorrow? Kennedy didn't even know what day it was. The bomb, the lockdown — how much time had passed? Had she slept a whole day through? Maybe more? Heavy plastic curtains were drawn on all sides of her bed. There were no windows, no clocks. It could just as easily be suppertime Monday night or first thing Wednesday morning or the middle of the night a week later.

Pain pulsed through her temples, behind her eyes, pounding on her optical nerves. She just wanted to sleep. Forget. Wake up in the morning in the Lindgrens' guest room to find this entire ordeal had been a terrible dream.

The nurse fidgeted with Kennedy's throbbing arm, adjusting some sort of a bandage. "You just rest up now and try not to worry."

Try not to worry? After everything she had gone through? The epidemic. The lockdown. The explosion...

"Where's Dominic?"

The nurse's face was completely shielded through the thick visor of her hazmat suit.

"The chaplain," Kennedy pressed. "He was there, too. When can I see him?" Her lungs clenched off, and she coughed trying to force a breath.

"Just calm down now, ok? There's a detective waiting to talk to you. He'll fill you in on everything that happened, and I know he's got some questions for you too. There's no rush, though. He said he'd wait as long as he needed until you felt like talking."

"I'm ready now."

Kennedy felt rather than saw the nurse frown at her. "You just woke up. It might be a good idea to save your strength."

"I'll talk to the detective. Answer any questions he's got."

"You've got some shrapnel in your arm. Cuts on your shoulder. Bruises and burns."

"I said I'll talk to him now."

"Ok." The nurse's voice was uncertain, but she pulled back one of the curtains and pointed to the tall man standing on the other side of a thick window. "This is Detective Drisklay. Says you already know him."

"Yeah." Kennedy's voice was flat. The nurse was probably right. She should have slept some more before voluntarily hopping into the witness chair with someone like Drisklay. He held up a Styrofoam coffee cup in silent greeting.

"There's a phone by your bedside you can use to talk to him through the glass. You sure you're up for this?" the nurse asked one last time.

Kennedy swallowed. She had to find out what happened to Dominic.

"I'm ready."

CHAPTER 23

"I hear they expect you to recover from your injuries." Drisklay stared through Kennedy's window.

She rested the hospital phone against her ear so she wouldn't have to hold it in place. "Yeah, it's nothing too serious, I guess. How's Dominic?"

"What can you tell me about Brian Robertson?" Drisklay went on as if he hadn't heard Kennedy's question. Was the mouthpiece of her phone working?

She tried to remember what details she could give the detective. "He had a son. He was upset about the court order." Kennedy squeezed her eyes shut, trying not to think about the young cancer patient. About how much sorrow the poor boy had already endured in his short life. About how horrific it must be for him to learn about what his father had done.

"We know about the son." Drisklay took a sip out of his Styrofoam cup so noisily Kennedy could hear it through her phone. "We want to piece together what happened in the conference room. My coffee is just now kicking in, so you may as well start at the beginning."

Kennedy's thoughts were too disorganized, her brain too stunned for her to put her words into any coherent order.

"He had a vest. A bomb. With his phone."

"When did you meet him?" Drisklay interrupted. "How long had you been in that room with him before he decided to blow himself to bits?"

"I don't know."

"Was he holding you hostage?"

"No. I mean, I'm not sure. He locked the door so I couldn't get out."

"So he was holding you hostage."

"He didn't want to hurt me."

"Which is why he lit himself off like a firework? You're one lucky young woman. You know that, don't you?"

Lucky? She doubted her definition of the word would match the detective's very closely.

"Did he say anything about any other explosives? Did he make any other threats?" Drisklay spoke in his regular monotone, but Kennedy could tell by the way he clenched his coffee cup that he was tense.

"No, the one he was wearing, that was the only bomb he mentioned."

"And not a very strong one," Drisklay added as an afterthought. His words gave Kennedy a small boost of hope.

"What about Dominic?"

The detective frowned. "Who?"

"The chaplain." Her abs quivered. Even though she was reclining in the hospital bed, every single muscle in her body engaged at the same time.

"Martinez?" He shrugged. "You're lucky he was there. Lucky he put his training to good use. Puny as the explosive was, you still would have been obliterated if Martinez hadn't tackled Mr. Robertson. Absorbed eighty percent of the blast or more." Drisklay nodded appreciatively. "Smart thinking."

Kennedy wished the curtains on either side of her were open. She was suffocating in this cramped enclosure. She had to breathe. Had to find room for her lungs to expand. She tried to sit up, but the pain in her arm and shoulder was too intense. "What happened to him, then?" She stared at Drisklay's expressionless face, searching, pleading, begging for any trace of softness or sympathy.

He took another noisy gulp of coffee. "Who, Martinez? Let's just say the chaplain's legacy and sacrifice will go down in history. It's because of him that you and everyone else in the west corridor are alive and not in gallon-sized biohazardous waste baggies."

Legacy? Sacrifice? Did that mean ...

Drisklay shrugged. "Just be thankful it was one of our men and not someone you knew personally. Be thankful you're safe and forget what anyone tells you about survivor's guilt or myths like that."

Was Drisklay really saying what she thought he was? She had to be imagining it. No creature could be that callous.

"Just how bad was it?" She had to know.

Drisklay took another sip from his cup. "Let's just say the chaplain will be getting a hero's funeral, but it won't be open-casket."

CHAPTER 24

Tears. Somewhere behind Kennedy's dry eyes were tears. Someplace beneath her shocked psyche was a grief that would threaten to carry her down to the pit of despair. Angry. Demanding God tell her why he took Dominic away. Devastated. Wondering how she could find healing after a loss like this.

But right now, there was nothing. The numbness was so tangible, so fierce even her limbs felt cold. Unmoving. Had her circulatory system shut down entirely?

Beep. Beep.

The hospital monitor mocked her, reminding her seventy-two times a minute that she was alive. That she still had a pulse. That there was nowhere for her to go but forward. Forward without him. Without what could have been.

He'd died for her. Wasn't that supposed to make her feel something? Guilty? Thankful? Wretched?

Beep. Beep.

She would never see him again. No more Sunday morning walks through Boston Commons. No more late-night phone calls asking him her most recent theological musings.

No more Dominic.

Beep. Beep.

And yet Kennedy lived on.

Beep.

Her heart pumped blood. Her lungs took in oxygen, albeit in short, shallow bursts.

Beep.

And she felt nothing at all.

CHAPTER 25

She didn't know how long it had been since Detective Drisklay left when the phone by her bedside rang. There was nobody in the window in front of her room. Who was calling?

She reached her uninjured arm across her body and winced as she tried to pick up the receiver. "Hello?"

"Kennedy, sweetheart, thank God I got hold of you." Sandy's voice was breathless. Constantly bustling, just like her. "The nurses told me you were awake now. Has the detective come by, hon? I really want to talk to you before he gets …"

"Yeah. We already talked."

"Oh." Her chipper voice fell flat. "So, he told you then?"

"Yeah. He told me."

"Baby, I'm so, so sorry. I wish I could come over there and give you a big hug. You know that, don't you? You know I would if it weren't for the isolation rules, right?"

"Yeah."

"Talk to me, precious. Tell me what you're thinking. You don't need to keep things bottled up, you know. Tell me everything. You know I'm always here for you."

Kennedy's throat seized up. She loved Sandy, but talking to her pastor's wife on a hospital phone was no substitute for burying herself in her mother's arms and crying. Releasing all that fear. That tension. That sorrow that hadn't yet even crept up into her spirit. It was there, buried somewhere beneath the surface. She couldn't access it now even if she wanted to. She felt as callous as Detective Drisklay himself. So unfeeling.

So homesick.

"What are you thinking, baby?"

Kennedy bit her lip. If Sandy kept on talking to her with so much compassion, so much concern, she'd start crying. And once she started ...

"I'm ok. I'm just glad more people weren't hurt, you know?"

"Well, yes. We're all praising God for that, I'm sure. But honey, you know what I'm asking about. I'm talking about Dominic. You do know that he ..."

"Yeah. The detective told me."

"Honey, I'm so sorry. I begged the nurses to let me talk to you first. I thought maybe ..." Sandy's voice caught. "I thought maybe it'd be easier for you coming from me. I'd come right in that room and hold you if they'd let me. You know that, right?"

"Uh-huh."

"How you feeling, babe? Your injuries, are they pretty bad?"

God bless Sandy. It was infinitely easier to talk about her physical wounds. "My arm hurts a lot. And my shoulder. But it's nothing too serious."

Thanks to Dominic, she added silently. What was that verse in John? *Greater love has no one that this ...*

She couldn't think about it. Not right now.

"Are you ok?" Kennedy hated herself for not asking sooner. "How's Woong? And what about Carl? Is he all right?"

"Carl and I are fine, precious. In fact, he's right here." Sandy lowered her voice. "Here, babe. Say hi to Kennedy for a minute. It's been a rough day for her."

"It's been a rough day for all of us," came the pleasant-sounding grumble.

"Carl?" Kennedy wasn't sure he'd picked up the phone yet or if he was still bantering with his wife.

"Kennedy." His voice boomed. She was grateful to hear the strength in his tone. "Hey, next time we ask you to babysit our son, I promise not to do it in the middle of an epidemic, all right?"

She smiled. "Sounds good."

"Let's plan to avoid any more hospital lockdowns while we're at it, ok?" Good old Carl. Ready to remind Kennedy that joy still existed in spite of terror and heartache. Reminding her that one day she too would find courage to laugh again.

"Are you all right?" she asked. "We were really worried about you. All I heard was Sandy was driving you to the ER."

"Pshaw. I'm fine. You know me. God's not about to call me home yet. Not with all the work he's still got left for me to do."

"What was wrong?" Was it rude for her to ask? Should she have worded the question more delicately?

Carl chuckled. "Well, turns out that being fifty pounds overweight and snacking on my lovely wife's cookies and muffins for decades was enough to kill my pancreas, that's all."

"What?"

"He's got diabetes, hon," Sandy's voice rang out in the background.

"Oh. Is it serious?"

"Not very," Carl answered.

"His blood sugar levels were 485 when we admitted him."

"I'll be fine," Carl thundered. "Like I said, God's not even close to finished with me yet, and when it's my time to go, there isn't a soul in a hundred miles who could stop me. But until then, the devil can try to take me all he wants, but God's not through with me, and I'm just gonna keep on giving him glory."

"Except now you'll be giving him glory with diet and exercise," Sandy added.

"Woman, we got more important things to worry about right now than my insulin levels. Listen, first we get Woong over this infection, we get ourselves home as a family again, and then we'll talk about my diet. Promise. Here. You take the phone again. I'm about to die of thirst. These hospital meals ..." His voice trailed off, and Sandy came back on the line.

"You still there, pumpkin? Sorry about that." She lowered her voice. "He's an ornery patient. Just ask his nurses."

"I heard that." There was laughter in Carl's tone. Laughter that squeezed Kennedy's heart between her ribs and sent pangs piercing through her spirit with the intensity of the nuclear explosion at the end of *Armageddon*.

"Did they say when they're going to let you out of isolation?" Sandy asked.

"Tomorrow night if I don't show any symptoms."

"That's good. It's the same with me and Carl."

"You're in isolation, too?"

"Oh, yeah. It's horrible, isn't it? When I should be there taking care of Woong. But they've got us two rooms right next to each other, and speakers so you don't even have to use phones to talk. And the nurses, they're letting him play XBox when he's got the energy for it, so he's the happiest little patient in the history of Providence Hospital. When he's awake," she added quietly.

"How is he? Is he really sick?"

"We're still waiting on his test results, hon." Sandy's voice betrayed her heaviness for the first time since they started talking. "Waiting and trusting in the good Lord to do what's right. His teacher turns out to have a bad case of meningitis, but at least it's not related to Nipah, so there's hope there. It just breaks my mother's heart thinking about all the things it could be, so I'm trying to focus on the fact that right now, right at this minute, Carl and me are together, and our son's right next to us. He's sleeping now, but when he wakes up, he'll want nothing more than to play his silly racing games, big grin on his face. His fever's down just a tad. So until the doctors tell me it's time to worry, I'm sitting here counting my blessings."

"That's nice that you and Carl get to be by him." Kennedy would give just about anything to have her parents with her right now, even if she could only see them through the glass.

"Oh, we wouldn't have it any other way. At first, they wanted to split us all up. When the bomb scare went off, they would have just evacuated, you know. Sent everyone home except for the patients and workers who couldn't leave. But by then, Woong had come down with this fever all of a sudden. We told them he was one of the students in Mrs. Winifred's class, and that was before they got her test results in, so they realized they couldn't just send everyone away. You should have seen the flurry over here. Running and racing and figuring out who'd been in contact with Woong. Once they got it sorted, they let most folks out, but a few of us they had to put in isolation. Problem was they wanted to keep us as far away from the ER as possible, back when they still thought the bomb was in there, and there weren't enough isolation rooms for everyone. So me and Carl, we just told them to put us together. We said if our son's sick, well, we'd rather all be sick together, come what may, than stand back and watch each other suffer from a distance. I just wish they'd found a way to put all three of us together, but that has as much to do with Carl still needing a hospital bed as anything else. He won't tell you this himself, but he's still hooked up to IVs. Still working to get his blood sugar under control."

Kennedy was glad Carl and Sandy were together. But she couldn't figure out how Sandy could be so happy with her son so ill. Well, maybe she wasn't exactly happy, but if Kennedy had been in her place, she would have been freaking out. Screaming, pleading with God to save her son's life. Begging every doctor and nurse in the entire country to do what they could to help him.

Of course, she'd never go so far as murder, but she thought she understood a little more clearly what must have been running through Brian Robertson's head when he strapped himself with explosives and walked into Providence Hospital.

"Well, I'm sure I've yacked your ear off by now, but you can call whenever you want to chat. I mean it, I don't care what time it is. You call, and I'll be here for you." She let out a pleasant, ringing chuckle. "It's not like I'll be going anywhere any time soon."

"Thank you." Kennedy wished her weary spirit could

feel the gratitude she knew Sandy deserved. She winced again when she reached over to hang up the phone. She still didn't know what time it was. Still didn't know how many more hours she had to go to find out if she'd caught Woong's disease or not. She didn't know if grief would overtake her now or if it'd take weeks before her soul could fully realize everything she'd lost in the past twenty-four hours.

All she knew was that she was tired. And that she wanted to sleep for a very long time.

CHAPTER 26

"Well, you'll be glad to hear you're in picture-perfect shape." The nurse pulled the thermometer out of Kennedy's mouth and took off her hazmat mask. "I'll get that bandage changed for you one last time and bring you some gauze so you can take care of it at home. After that, you're free as a sparrow."

Kennedy let out her breath. She hadn't caught Nipah. No fever. No aches besides the ones that could be explained from the explosion. The explosion and the gnawing, gaping wound in her spirit.

"Well look at that," the nurse prattled pleasantly. "Looks like you already have your first visitor." She took off her enormous gloves and held the door open. "Come in. Come in. You're right on time, and she's just gotten her clean bill of health."

Kennedy looked at Willow standing in the open doorway and offering a smile, somewhat less certain than her usual brilliant grin.

"Hey."

"Hey."

The girls stared at each other before Willow finally asked, "Can I come in?"

"Yeah. I'm not sick or anything."

"Me either."

"They kept you in isolation?"

"Only for the first night. I would have been wicked bored, too, except I had someone to talk to."

Kennedy could tell she was trying hard to hide a grin. "Oh, yeah? Who was that?"

"Just your friend Nick. Man, if I'd have known the youth pastor had such gorgeous hair and an even hotter personality, I would have been begging you to take me to church for the past two years. Oh, and did you know his uncle's in a band? It's wicked awesome. You should listen to their album. But enough about that." Willow sat down on the foot of Kennedy's bed. "How are you doing? I heard about everything. You must feel terrible."

"Yeah, something like that."

"I'm not trying to make you feel worse. I mean, I don't even know what Christians are supposed to say at times like this. Do you?"

Kennedy shook her head.

197

"Well, I started thinking about your pastor and his family and how you said when the lockdown started they were probably all in their room together praying. I figured that even if I was completely clueless when it came to finding the right things to say, I could at least offer to do that with you, right? I mean, you don't have to say anything unless you really want to. And you know me. I'm still learning all the stuff, so I probably won't even do that good of a job with it, but I'll be happy to pray with you if that's what you want."

Kennedy swallowed past the painful lump in her throat and nodded slightly.

Willow scooted closer to her on the bed. "So, like, are we supposed to hold hands or something? Does that make it better, or do we just sit here or what, because I really don't want to mess up after all you've been through."

"It doesn't matter." Kennedy squeezed her eyes shut. Felt the first trickle of a tear starting to form.

"Ok. So if it doesn't make a difference how we do it, maybe you can just sit here, and I'll like rub your back or something, unless it feels strange to you. It's ok for me to do that, right? Doesn't weird you out?"

Kennedy didn't trust her voice, so she shook her head.

"All right. I'm gonna pray for you now. So, God, or Father, whichever you prefer, we're here, and Kennedy's heartbroken, I'm sure, and she's gone through more than anybody should have to endure in an entire lifetime. And even though she probably thinks she's just one big mess, you and I both know how strong she is. How brave of a person she is. How much faith and courage it takes to go through everything she's gone through and still have the confidence to say, 'I believe in a good and loving God who knows how to take care of his children.' So that's what I'm asking right now, Lord. Or Jesus. I'm asking you to show Kennedy that she's stronger than she thinks, and she's braver than she feels right now, and even when she feels like she's nothing but a big screw-up, or I mean... Well, Lord, you know exactly what it is I mean. And even though what happened to her boyfriend sucks royally — or stinks, I guess that's a better way of putting it — I'm asking you to please just teach my friend here what she taught me earlier, that you won't even let a sparrow get hurt without knowing about it in advance and saying it's going to be ok. So please help Kennedy remember right now that you've got her whole life planned out, and I know you have so many good things in store for her even if she can't feel or believe in them now."

Willow continued to rub Kennedy's back. "There, was that ok? Do I say *amen* next, or does God just know when I'm done, or do you have to do the whole *in Jesus name* thing, or can you do whatever? I spent a lot of time thinking about what I was going to pray, so I want to make sure it gets through."

Kennedy wanted to assure Willow that her prayer was perfectly acceptable, but she couldn't find her voice through her trembling and her silent, crippling sobs.

CHAPTER 27

"Want me to buckle you in?" Willow asked.

Kennedy lowered herself carefully into the passenger seat of her roommate's car. "No, I can get it." She grimaced as she twisted around to grab the seatbelt.

"You've got to learn to accept a little help sometimes, you know." Willow plopped into the driver's seat and started up the engine.

Kennedy smiled. "Maybe next semester."

Willow rolled her eyes. "Maybe after the apocalypse, you mean. Wait, is that a real thing? Is that like actually in the Bible? Do I need to do anything to get ready for it?"

"It's in the Bible, but maybe we can save that topic for later." Kennedy held her breath as Willow bounced the car over a speed bump and pulled out of the hospital parking lot. The sun was just starting to set, glorious hues of pink and orange highlighting the oversized cumulus clouds.

It felt so good to finally be out of Providence.

"I talked to your pastor's wife," Willow said. "She made

me promise to find you something nutritious for dinner on campus and make sure you get some good rest and actually go to sleep. I don't remember entirely. I think there might have been something about tucking you in and kissing you goodnight too."

Kennedy smiled through her pain. "Thanks for being with me."

"Hey, what are friends for? Besides, if it hadn't been for you, I would have never met Nick."

"I thought you were going to say without me you would have never met Jesus."

"Oh, well, there's that too. But Nick ... Man. Why didn't you tell me about him years ago?"

Kennedy let out an awkward chuckle. Would she ever remember what it felt like to laugh naturally? She took in a deep breath, thankful for the fresh air whipping across her face.

Willow turned up the radio so they could hear the music over the breeze roaring in through the open windows as they sped toward campus. "Please don't tell me I have to give up my classic rock station now that I'm a Christian."

Kennedy wasn't sure if she was serious or not.

They listened in silence. *Here I Go Again on my Own.* Ironic song choice now that Dominic was gone. Except

Kennedy wasn't alone. She had Willow, her best friend and sister in the Lord. She had Carl and Sandy, who had thankfully both been released from isolation and cleared of any Nipah scare. She had her mom and dad, even though they were on the other side of the world. From the time she woke up in Providence, not an hour had gone by where at least one of her parents hadn't called to check in on her. Smother her with love and care. It didn't bother Kennedy at all. She didn't even mind when her dad told her she should check her temperature a few times during the night just to make sure she really hadn't caught whatever Woong had.

Poor Woong. Kennedy and Willow had stopped to check on him before they headed back to campus. Whatever energy he'd found to play Xbox earlier was clearly expended. When Kennedy went over to visit, he was lying half-awake in bed while Sandy read him the last chapter of *The Boxcar Children* through the window of his room. Even though Carl and Sandy had been cleared, the doctors were still holding Woong in quarantine until his test results came back.

There were so many things Kennedy had to worry about, had to process. She was glad she wouldn't be spending the night alone. She would have been infinitely more comfortable at the Lindgrens' than at her dorm, but with Woong being so sick, nobody was allowed into their house until they found out if he really had Nipah or not.

"What do you want to have for dinner?" Willow asked. "You know you have to eat more than your usual craisins and Cheerios."

Kennedy didn't want to think about anything. "We'll figure something out when we get to campus."

"What do you want to do after that? It's not that late. We could watch a movie or play some cards or take a little walk. It's a nice evening."

It felt so wrong to be here. Sitting next to her friend, the wind whipping through their hair. The sunset so soul-hauntingly glorious. So intense. The kind of scene you'd expect to see on a postcard or movie trailer. Not in real life.

The world was so stinking beautiful. But ever since she'd learned about Dominic's death, Kennedy's soul had been longing for those things to come. That glorious rapture, that heavenly melody that would one day beckon to her as it had to her boyfriend.

When Jesus is my portion; my constant friend is he.
His eye is on the sparrow, and I know he watches me.

She'd heard her whole life that heaven was her true home, but she never fully realized what that meant until now.

"Well? What sounds good?" Willow interrupted her thoughts, her voice full of forced cheer. "We could even call

Nick and invite him over if you feel up for some company. I bet he'd be willing to pick us up a pizza from Angelo's or something."

Kennedy knew exactly what Willow was doing. Trying to distract her. Trying to keep her mind off the pain. Off the loss.

Reminding her that life on earth was here for the living. Heaven was the prize for those who had already passed.

CHAPTER 28

Kennedy woke up the next morning to the sound of rain pounding on her dorm room window.

Her roommate was reclining in her beanbag chair reading a screenplay. "Morning, sleeping beauty."

Kennedy glanced at the clock. Already past ten.

"How're you doing today?" Willow set down her book.

How was she doing? Kennedy wasn't sure yet.

"Your dad called. Twice." Willow smiled. "I told him you were perfectly fine. He wants you to check your temperature and text him."

"Ok." Her dad annoyed her ninety percent of the time, but today, she was glad to know someone was worried for her. Someone was still there to fret and fawn over her every move.

"Sandy called too. She said that Woong's been asking for you. Wants you to read to him if you've got the energy. I told her you might not want to go back to the hospital just yet, and she said she understood." Willow frowned. "Is that ok? I wasn't sure what to say."

"I don't know." Kennedy glanced around. She was still more thirsty than usual. Her arm ached, but it was nothing compared to yesterday. She would heal. She would recover. She hadn't looked beneath the bandage yet. Didn't know if she'd end up scarred or not from the shrapnel.

Did it matter?

She tugged at her sleeve. "If Woong wants me there, I don't mind." It was nice feeling needed. Surrounding herself with people who loved her. Who wanted her around.

Willow shrugged. "I can give you a ride."

"That'd be nice."

"Hey, you want some tea? I just heated some up."

"Thanks." Kennedy reached out and took the oversized *Alaska Chicks Rock* mug. The steam heated her face. She sensed Willow staring at her. Kennedy hated the sad, almost embarrassed expression in her eyes. She just wanted to move on. How long until she could forget this week? How long until she could look at her roommate without seeing that pained, guilty expression?

Life would go on. Kennedy knew it would. She just wished she had some idea how.

Half an hour later, after a quick bite from L'Aroma Bakery, Kennedy and Willow made their way back to Providence.

"All I can say is Woong must be a very special little boy if you're willing to go back to the hospital to see him."

Kennedy couldn't explain. It wasn't just Woong. She loved him. Prayed that God would heal him of whatever sickness he had. But it was more than that. She wanted to be with the Lindgrens. To support and encourage each other. Carl and Sandy needed her, and she needed them. The Lindgrens were the closet thing Kennedy had to a family in the States, and during her own time of sadness and mourning, she wanted to be with family most of all.

Besides, this was the morning they would get Woong's lab results back from the CDC. If it really was the Nipah virus, Kennedy wanted to be with Sandy. Help shoulder some of that burden like Sandy had done for her countless times over the past two years. She thought about her first week on US soil when she arrived for the start of her freshman year at Harvard. How much she'd seen since then. How much she'd grown.

How much she'd changed.

She wasn't sure all the changes were positive, either. Kennedy lived now with a constant heaviness, a sense of fear even when she knew she was perfectly safe. That little bubble, that sense she'd had as a child that she was completely invincible, popped within her first few weeks of college. She'd never be able to recreate that same sense of security.

But still, God had sustained her. Carried her through every trial she'd had to endure. He'd given her strength when she was so weak she was sure she'd collapse. He'd sent heavenly protection to shield her when she was sure she was about to die. He'd shown her love, the kind of love you couldn't read about in a book. Sacrificial love. Christ-like love.

And he'd shown her comfort. Kennedy couldn't feel it right now, but she had in the past and knew that it would come to her again. She'd have to learn to be patient, that was all. The comfort would come, that sweet heavenly balm that would smooth over her scars. It would never erase them completely. She'd given up praying for perfect healing, but she knew that in time, the pain would lessen. Joy would find her once more. Teach her to smile again. Hope again.

Love again.

It would happen. She just had to be patient. That was the hardest part, but God would give her the grace even for that.

"What are you thinking about?" Willow turned down the radio. Rain pelted onto the windshield and splashed up from the car tires in front of them.

"Everything."

"Yeah." Willow sighed. "Me, too." She reached out and shut off the music. "Hey, can I ask you something?"

"What?" Kennedy was thankful for the chance she'd had this week to connect with Willow on a deeper level. To discuss the spiritual matters they should have been talking about from the moment of Willow's conversion. But she was so tired. She didn't know if she could focus on a heavy conversation right now.

"I'm still wondering about sickness and prayer and all that stuff. I mean, I'm thinking about Woong, I guess. And I know you said even a bird won't get hurt outside of God's plans, but ... I don't even know how to ask my question. I guess what I'm wanting to know ... It doesn't make sense to me ..."

"How God chooses to heal some people and not others?" Kennedy finished for her.

"Right. How exactly does that work?"

Kennedy sighed. "I wish I could tell you." She knew Willow was hoping for a deeper answer than that, so she tried to snap her mind into a more alert state. "I think it's kind of like ... Ok, so let's say that ..." She wasn't going to be able to get out one coherent sentence without the Holy Spirit's intervention. "It's like this," she tried again. "At least, I think it is, because I'm definitely not an expert. But let's say someone you love is sick. Use Woong as an example, right?"

"Right." Willow sped up her windshield wipers.

"Ok, so we're all praying for Woong to get better. I mean, who wouldn't be?"

"Right."

"So we all want him to get better." Kennedy had to pause for a moment. She couldn't imagine the grief that would flood the Lindgren household if Woong didn't recover. "We want him to get well, and so we pray for him, and that's the right thing to do. But there's more to it than just that. Like when Jesus was in the Garden of Gethsemane. Do you know that story?"

"Gethsemane? Sounds like the name of a big music festival."

"I guess. Well, that's where Jesus went to pray the night before he was crucified. I mean killed. He's praying there, and he says, *God, please don't let me have to die, but it's not what I will, but what you will.* So he was praying to God for his own desires, but then he also started to pray that if God wanted something different, that should be what happens instead. Does that make sense?"

"No. Because if Jesus is God, why would he pray to himself?"

Kennedy sighed. She couldn't think through everything logically right now. "Ok, that's a whole other question we can talk about a different time." She was just about to make a mental note to ask Dominic how he would answer that when she remembered. She wondered how long it would take before she fully realized he was gone. It was like losing a limb but for weeks, even months, you keep trying to use it. Keep surprising yourself when you rediscovered it isn't there. Mourn its loss all over again.

She tried to remember Willow's original question. "Well, with God, we should pray like Jesus did. We can tell him what's on our hearts, what we want out of the situation, but there should also be the submission to recognize that he might know better — he *does* know better — and that even if he doesn't answer our prayers the way we expect him too, we still have to have faith that he's good."

"So basically, you're saying that if Woong's gonna die, Woong's gonna die, and that God has some sort of good reason for making that happen. So then why do we pray for his healing at all?"

She didn't have an answer. Where was Dominic when she needed him? Why couldn't he be here to tackle these questions for her? Why did God take him the way he did? Did Kennedy even believe everything she was telling

Willow? Did God actually *want* Dominic to die, or did he just choose not to intervene when some lunatic took his life? She let out her breath. "I really don't know. Prayer's important. I just don't know ..." She let her voice trail off before apologizing. "I wish I had more to tell you."

Willow slowed down to turn into the Providence parking garage. "That's ok. I guess I probably picked a bad time to come up with heavy questions like that. I'm sorry. I know you have other things on your mind right now."

"Don't feel bad. I love that you're asking these things. It's just that ..." Her voice caught. "He was always so much better at theology than me."

Willow reached out and rubbed Kennedy's leg. "I know."

Kennedy swallowed and reminded herself it wouldn't always be so painful. Right now, she had other things to think about. Like Woong and his parents.

Willow parked, and the girls walked into the hospital without talking. Kennedy was thankful Willow didn't try to fill the silence with empty words or platitudes. She was thankful her friend knew her well enough to leave her to her own thoughts for a while. When Kennedy was ready to talk, when she was ready to laugh and play and live again, Willow would be there for her. And she was with her now, right beside her on the way to Woong's hospital room. Right next to her as Kennedy fought through the trembling in her gut.

Sandy was in the hall, leaning against the window and talking into the phone outside the quarantine chamber. She smiled tiredly when she saw Kennedy and Willow. "Good morning, girls." She wrapped Kennedy up in a sturdy hug. "I love you, sweetie. I've been praying for you all morning. You and Woong. That's about all God's heard from me today, I'm afraid."

Willow held back when her phone beeped.

"How's Carl?" Kennedy glanced around looking for him.

"He's doing a lot better. Got himself discharged last night. And good thing, too. He was about to drive those nurses crazy."

Kennedy smiled. "How's his health?"

"Got his sugar levels under two-hundred. Praise the Lord for that. He'll be on meds for it. Have to change the way he eats, which means less sweets. I either need to find some new recipes or come up with a new hobby." She twirled a strand of gray hair that had fallen out of her braid. "But listen to me prattle. Are you all right, hon? Did you sleep ok?"

Kennedy nodded.

"And your roommate? She's taking good care of you?"

Kennedy glanced over at Willow, who was laughing at an incoming text. "Yeah. She's been great."

"I'm so glad you two have each other."

Kennedy had to agree. Leave it to Sandy to help her focus on her blessings even in the midst of such turmoil.

"How's Woong today?"

Sandy sighed. "I don't know, pumpkin. I just don't know. One minute he's fine. Playing Xbox, wanting me to read to him. Next thing, his fever spikes, and he can't even hold his head up. It's a sad business, darling, to see your own child that sick." She shook her head. "I feel so bad, dear. You're going through your own storms all by yourself, and I've been too worried to do you any good, I'm afraid."

"No, you've been great." Kennedy wanted to give Sandy another hug but felt self-conscious about it. Usually, Sandy was the one hugging her. "And I hope you know we're praying hard for Woong. Willow and me both."

"Well, I appreciate it, love. That boy needs all the prayer covering he can get."

Kennedy wanted to ask Sandy the same question Willow had asked her on the way to Providence, but it wasn't the right time.

A nurse stepped up behind Sandy and tapped her on the shoulder. "Excuse me, Mrs. Lindgren. The doctor told me they have your son's test results back. They're waiting for you in the conference room."

Sandy smoothed out the fabric of her flowery skirt. "Oh, that soon? Oh, dear. Let me just tell Woong I need to step out for a minute ..."

"He's asleep." The nurse pointed through the window.

"Ok, that's good. Poor little angel hardly slept a wink last night. Now, I just need to wait for my husband. He stepped into the men's room down the hall. I doubt he'll be ..."

"My supervisor already found him. He's at the conference room. They're just waiting for you."

Sandy gave Kennedy a nervous smile. "Oh, then I guess I better go. You don't mind waiting here in case he wakes up, do you, sweetie? I hate the thought of him all alone in there, finding everyone gone, all by himself in that big room ..."

"I'll stay here," Kennedy assured her.

Sandy gave her a weak half-hug. "Then I guess I'll be back."

Kennedy thought she felt Sandy's body quiver just a little.

"I'll see you then."

Sandy offered a brave smile then turned around, her long skirt rustling around her as she followed the nurse down the hall to hear her son's prognosis.

CHAPTER 29

Kennedy had never spent a longer fifteen minutes. Once Willow finished texting, Kennedy filled her in on what was going on, and they both decided it was time to join together in prayer. A few minutes later, after praying through every possible outcome and every possible contingency they could collectively imagine, there was nothing to do but wait.

"Nick wants to know if you want to swing over to his house tonight. He's making spaghetti and says we can play some cards afterwards. I told him I'd only go if you feel up to it."

Kennedy could hardly focus on her words. How long would those doctors take?

"Sure, that sounds fun."

"You don't have to decide right now. We can always play it by ear."

"Yeah, ok."

"You don't have a clue what I'm talking about, do you?"

"I'm listening."

"What did I just say?"

"Something about tonight. You want to play cards."

Willow gave Kennedy's uninjured shoulder a reassuring squeeze. "It's going to be ok. You'll see." She smiled. "I've got a good feeling about this."

Kennedy doubted that Willow's positive outlook made any real difference, but she was thankful at least one of them was optimistic. Kennedy wished she could bottle up and borrow some of that hope.

"I'm serious. I don't know how to explain it. But a few minutes ago, back when we were praying for Woong, I got this really settled feeling in my heart. Like someone was reaching out and letting me know it's going to be just fine. Do you think that was God? I mean, does he work that way? Or do I have my signals crossed?"

Kennedy tried to smile. "I really don't know. I guess it might have been the Lord."

"Yeah, your pastor, he was saying something like that in his sermon last Sunday."

Kennedy studied her quizzically. "Saying something like what?"

"That God can talk to you through the Holy Spirit. What'd he call it? A still, small voice. Something like that."

"You went to Saint Margaret's?"

Willow stared at her neon-green fingernails. "No, but I listened to the sermon online while I was doing my yoga the other day. What are you looking at me like that for?"

"I didn't know you were listening to any sermons."

Willow shrugged. "Gotta learn somewhere, right? He's a pretty good preacher, you know."

"Yeah," Kennedy sighed. "He really is."

"So anyway," Willow went on, "what do you think about what I was saying? Think that really was God talking to me? Telling me everything was going to be fine?"

Kennedy didn't want to discourage her friend, but she didn't want Willow to get her hopes up too high only to be disappointed, either. "I don't know. It could have been anything. Could have been God, could have been wishful thinking ..."

"No, this was different. There was something ... I don't know. Something special about this. I'm new to all this Christian stuff, you know, but I really don't think it was me making it all up. Does that make any sense?"

"I guess so. Who knows? Maybe it really was God talking to you, telling you Woong would be ok."

"I hope so. But like you said, who knows, right? I mean, God probably lets lots of things happen to you all the time without giving you warning, right?"

Kennedy stared blankly into Woong's quarantine room, the deafening thunder of Brian Robertson's explosives still echoing in her mind.

"No, you don't often get a warning."

CHAPTER 30

"Good news, girls!"

Kennedy had been so lost in thought that Sandy's chipper voice startled her.

Good news? Kennedy was ready for a heavy dose of that.

Willow elbowed her gently in the side. "See? What did I tell you?"

Sandy bustled up to Kennedy and Willow and gave them both giant hugs. "Oh, the Lord is good. The Lord is so good!"

"What'd you find out?" Kennedy asked.

Sandy let out a melodic chuckle. "Our son has typhus."

Kennedy stared, certain she'd heard wrong.

Willow paused with her fingers halfway through her hair. "I thought you just said …"

"It's not Nipah," Sandy interrupted joyously. "It's just plain old, regular typhus. Serious, of course, and it's a good thing they've had him in quarantine, but it's definitely treatable."

"How'd he catch it?" Kennedy asked.

"That's the funny thing. Well, not really funny. But the thing is, the doctors think he's already had typhus once. You know, he talked about falling real sick before he made his way to the orphanage. Back when he was still living on the streets. And we never knew what it was he had, but now the doctors think what happened was he caught typhus while he was still in Korea, recovered from it by the grace of God alone, and the infection he has now is basically a repeat of the same one. Something about the disease never completely leaving his system, and then it coming back up ... Oh, you'd have to ask the doctor for all the medical details. But what it means is it's perfectly treatable. I mean, poor thing'll have to stay in the hospital for a couple more days, but he'll be out of isolation soon. Won't have to sit in there all alone. I can be there with him, long as I wash up real good every time I leave and come back in. Have to wear a gown and whatnot, but at least we'll be together."

Kennedy didn't have to force her smile. Sandy's joy was wonderfully catching. "I'm so glad to hear that. You must be so relieved."

"Oh, you have no idea. I told God, I said to him, *Lord, I'm doing my hardest surrendering this boy to you, but God, I just can't give him up yet. I just can't.* And the whole time, there was something in me that knew. Knew I wasn't supposed to just roll over and accept this terrible illness. Knew I was supposed to pray for his healing and pray boldly. But I wasn't sure if that was coming from me or not. But I started out doing my best to surrender, surrender my child to the Lord just like Abraham on that mountain, and the more I prayed, the more I determined that God wanted me to pray that my little boy would be healed in Jesus' name. That I needed to go to battle for him and rebuke that sickness he had. I was so scared to believe it, but praise God, what really matters is Woong's going to be just fine. I'd invite you girls in to celebrate with us, but they still want to limit his contact with others. You'll excuse me if I'm rude and say good-bye for now, won't you? I just have to get in there and give my little boy a hug."

Kennedy glanced through the window, where Carl was already putting on the hospital's protective gear.

"You go in there," she told Sandy. "We'll talk to you soon."

Sandy blew a quick kiss and bustled through the door to the scrub station.

A few minutes later, Kennedy stood at the window and watched while Sandy scooped both arms beneath Woong and wrapped him up in a protective hug. Carl stood over them both, sobbing softly as he held his family close.

Kennedy blinked, surprised to find Willow's arm slipping around her.

"We should go," Willow whispered.

"Yeah," Kennedy agreed. She glanced once more at the emotional reunion, wondering if even heaven itself could contain that much joy, and then pried her eyes away. "Yeah, let's get out of here."

CHAPTER 31

"Well, this has been a great night so far. Anybody want some more spaghetti?" Nick held out the pot, which was almost completely empty.

"I'm stuffed," Kennedy admitted.

Willow hadn't stopped smiling at Nick. "Me, too."

They were seated around Nick's living room, which was surprisingly tidy compared to the other times Kennedy had been here.

Nick grabbed a deck of cards from his coffee table. "Who's up for a game?"

Willow glanced at Kennedy. "You tired, or should we stay for a little while?"

All Kennedy wanted to do was get to sleep, but she knew Willow would be disappointed if she didn't get a little more time with Nick. Kennedy had never seen two people connect as fast as they had. She didn't have a clue what happened while she was being held hostage in the conference room, but Nick and her roommate had already jumped past the awkward new-crush stage and were comfortably holding hands and making ridiculously goofy ga-ga faces at each other every chance they got. The picture was bittersweet. Kennedy was so happy her roommate had found someone, but still …

"Ok, you guys wanna play some rummy or hearts or Egyptian rat race?"

"What exactly is Egyptian rat race?" Kennedy asked.

"You mean you've never played?" Willow raised her penciled eyebrows incredulously.

"No. And I'm starting to think I'm the only person in Massachusetts who hasn't."

"You probably are." Nick explained the basic premise of the game. There was no way she could remember all the rules, but she was willing to give it a try. She glanced around his messy bachelor pad. At Willow's sappy smile. At Nick's shining eyes each time his hand brushed Willow's while he dealt out the cards.

So many good things had happened in the past few days. Woong's optimistic prognosis, at least compared to what it might have been if he'd really contracted the Nipah virus. Willow and Nick — apparently soulmates — finding each other in the chaos of a hospital lockdown. Willow's renewed interest in maturing her faith.

There was so much to be thankful for. So much joy around her. Kennedy wasn't about to burst into a belly laugh or forget the sorrows she'd experienced, but she could at least recognize and quietly rejoice in the happiness surrounding her.

She had no idea what the next few days and weeks would hold, but there was a peace in her spirit she couldn't deny. There would be tears. There would be grief. The heaviness of mourning. The weariness of sorrow. But through it all, the Lord would be with her. And so would her friends.

The comfort she felt wouldn't bring Dominic back to her, but somehow, she knew that it would be enough.

CHAPTER 32

Why should I feel discouraged,
Why should the shadows come,
Why should my heart be lonely,
And long for heaven and home,
When Jesus is my portion;
my constant friend is he.
His eye is on the sparrow,
and I know he watches me.

"That was wicked insane how many people showed up," Willow said as she and Kennedy followed the crowd out of the church.

"Yeah." If you included the photographers and members of the press eager to cover the funeral of Massachusetts' most recent hero, Kennedy guessed nearly a thousand people had shown up to pay their respects to the fallen chaplain.

"How are you doing?" Willow put her arm around Kennedy as the spring breeze whipped through their hair.

"A little better than I thought I would be. The service was really nice."

Willow nodded. "Yeah, it was. I like that last song they sang. What's that one called?"

"*His Eye is on the Sparrow.*"

"Yeah, that's a good one. It was fitting for today, too. Some of the others were so upbeat, it was like we were at some big fiesta instead of a funeral."

Kennedy didn't reply. As they crossed the street into Boston Commons, the spring sunshine warmed Kennedy's shoulders, soft and gentle heat streaming down on her from above.

"Hey, beautiful. Where are you speeding off to so fast?" Nick jogged up and pecked Willow on her cheek.

Kennedy glanced away when their fingers intertwined.

"Hey." Willow turned to look at Nick and kept her voice hardly above a whisper. "I think maybe we could use a few minutes. You know. Alone."

Nick nodded his head, his dreadlocks pumping up and down vigorously. "Yeah, I get it. Sure thing. Just don't forget I'm treating you both to Angelo's Pizza later on, right? We still up for that?"

"Yeah, I think so." Willow gave him a kiss. "I'll text you when we're ready."

Nick dashed off like a puppy who'd just been thrown a stick.

"You didn't have to send him away," Kennedy said. "I really don't mind. You two are adorable. It's like you were made for each other."

"Oh, I know. Just last night, we were talking about how we both ... Oh, never mind. You don't want to hear about that. Not on a day like this."

Kennedy didn't respond. Willow was right about one thing. Dominic's funeral had been lively and full of joy. Joy and pain at the same time. As she listened to the eulogies, she realized how much about him she'd never had the chance to learn. How much closer they could have grown. How much more they could have shared with each other if only God had given them more time. She couldn't explain how her heart could be so heavy but full of peace in the same instant. She thought about the first night she met Dominic, how his prayers for her had stopped her panic attack mid-sob. How heavenly healing had flowed from his intercession. If there was a common theme to any of the speeches made about Dominic today, it was his prayer life. Kennedy felt she could read a thousand books or listen to a thousand sermons on the subject and never come close to maturing into the kind of prayer warrior Dominic had been.

Had he known? That was Kennedy's biggest question, the one that kept her awake so many nights long after her tears and pillow both dried up. Had he known they would only be together for such a short time? Had he prayed for her? Had he prayed before the explosion that God would take care of her? Give her that sense of peace that had wrapped her up for the past week and a half?

Sure, there were tears. Not only at night, and sometimes at the most inappropriate times. Like when Willow made Nick laugh until Coke sprayed out his nose, and then Willow thought it was so funny she lost control and fell out of her chair. Kennedy pictured Dominic's expression if he had been there, that bemused, patient kindness softening his features even if he didn't join in the hilarity.

And she missed him.

She missed him when she went to St. Margaret's last Sunday instead of his cousin's home church and when the Christian radio station played his favorite hymn.

She missed him when Willow asked her difficult theological questions, like if God only has one person in mind that he wants you to marry or if there are several different options that would be good fits and it's up to you to make a wise decision.

She missed him when she looked out at the crowded

Boston Common, at the children trying to fly their kites around or chasing after soccer balls and Frisbees.

She missed him when she was awake.

And she missed him when she was asleep.

She missed him when she realized that now he was in heaven, reunited with his wife, worshiping in the presence of his Savior. Even if he had the ability to think about her down here at all, he'd have no real reason to.

"Hey! Hey, Kennedy!"

She slowed down at the sound of small tennis shoes plodding on the pavement behind her. She smiled down. "Hi, little buddy."

Woong was panting from running so hard. He still hadn't regained all his energy back after his illness, but he'd been symptom-free now for over a week. "I finally caught you," he said breathless. The warm sunshine lit up his cheeks, making him look strong and healthy.

"Did you enjoy the service?" she asked him.

"Uh-huh." Woong started walking alongside Kennedy.

She glanced back and spotted his parents to make sure they knew where he was. "What did you like about it?"

"When it was over. It got kinda long. Hey, you know that big box they had him in? It looked heavy, huh?"

"Yeah. It did."

"So that got me wondering, why do you think they make the box out of wood, I wonder? 'Cause back when people got the sickness in Korea, it weren't like they all got buried in wood like that. Sometimes it was just holes, know what I mean? And it got me thinking that maybe it wasn't so heavy when you do it that way, but it might get people upset, especially the ladies and little girls and ..."

"Ok," Willow interrupted, "maybe you should go find your parents so you guys don't get separated."

"Oh, I don't have to worry about that," Woong assured her. "Ever since I got out of the hospital, my mom won't leave me alone. One night, I even woke up, and guess who I saw sitting in a chair just staring at me? And I asked what she was doing there, and she said she was praying for me, and that got me wondering, why do you think she had to be in my room to pray for me? 'Cause I haven't read any of the Bible yet for myself, but my dad, he reads it tons, and he says you can pray to God anywhere. And you know he's gotta be telling the truth, him being a pastor and all."

Kennedy smiled. She'd take Woong's theological questions over discussions about caskets any day.

"So what I'm trying to figure out," he went on, "is why she had to be in my room to pray if God coulda heard her just as well in her own room. But I was still pretty sleepy-like on account of being so sick earlier, and that's why I hafta have an earlier bedtime now, at least until I get some of my energy back. And I lost a lot of weight in the hospital too, which is kinda funny if you think about it in a certain way. 'Cause my dad, you know he had to go to the hospital from having too much fat and calories and sugar and stuff and nonsense like that, so they put him in the hospital for those things. But me, they put me in the hospital, and now everyone's talking about how they want me to gain weight, not lose it like my dad has to. I told mom that means I should be able to get double desserts, ones for me like normal and then the ones my dad can't eat no more on account of him having the … oh, what's it called? Anchovies? No, that's not the right name. It's that thing with the sugar problem. You know what I'm talking about."

"Diabetes."

"Yeah, that. I don't know why, it always sounds like anchovies to me, but my mom says those are something else. She says there are some folks crazy enough to put fish on their pizza if you can believe that, but that's different from what my dad's got. But that reminds me. Mr. Nick, you know, he works with my dad. And he says that he really likes diabetes on his pizza because they're so salty." He turned to Willow. "But I bet you already know that, you being his new girlfriend and all. I think it's kinda funny if you ask me, 'cause two weeks ago the two of you didn't even know each other, and now you're kissing every minute or two. Once I seen you do it right on the lips when I bet you thought no one was looking."

"I'll make sure we're more careful next time." Willow scratched her cheek, and Kennedy thought she detected a hint of a blush.

"You better," Woong continued, "'cause that kissing, it's serious. Like my sister Blessing, she's got this son a little smaller than me and she's got an even tinier baby too, and so actually I'm their uncle which is pretty funny if you think about it, right? But she didn't get married until after Jayden started growing in her tummy, so I asked her how that worked when my mom and dad say you gotta be married before the babies come along and all, but she said she wasn't careful about who she kissed and that's how she ended up with my nephew. So all I'm saying is you and Mr. Nick better know what you're doing, 'cause you look a little too skinny for a baby to even fit in your belly, right?"

Willow couldn't control her laughter. "You run back to your parents now, ok?"

"All right. But before I go, there's something I wanted to give Kennedy." He reached into his pocket and pulled out a piece of paper folded up into a small rectangle. "Mom said you're probably gonna be sad for a while, with Mr. Dominic who's dead being your old boyfriend and all, so I asked her what she thought might cheer you up and she said this would probably do it. It's a picture I drawed. It's got a sunset, because I asked her and Mom said you always liked pictures of pretty sunsets. And then I told Mom I wanted a Bible verse on it, since whenever you come over and talk to her, she's always saying verses from the Bible and stuff and nonsense like that. So I told her to pick a Bible verse, but she wanted me to do it, so what we ended up doing was she gave me a few choices, and I picked from there. I wrote it myself too. Mom helped a little with the spelling is all."

Kennedy unfolded the page. "It's just perfect."

"Good, 'cause I was a little worried when Mom said I spelled *fatter* instead of *Father*. See? But I guess it's all right because you know what it's supposed to mean, don't you?"

Kennedy stared at the drawing. The sunset itself was crude at best, but she had to give Woong credit for his imaginative use of color. It was the first time she'd seen either purple or pea-green streaking across the sky, but there was enough orange and red to balance it out.

In the middle of the picture was a cloud with a verse scribbled on the inside. Kennedy might not have recognized all the words if she didn't already know the passage by heart. In fact, it had been quoted several times at Dominic's service.

Not even a sparrow falls to the ground apart from the will of your Father.

Woong reached out a finger and pointed to a few black M shapes by the clouds. "Them are the birds. You know, the sparrows it talks about."

"It's beautiful." She gave him a quick hug, and then he squirmed free and ran to his parents.

Willow glanced at the picture over her shoulder. "That's really sweet."

Kennedy had lost her voice and could only nod.

"You know, most girls just dream about being loved so much someone would be willing to die for them. You actually had it happen to you."

"He would have done it for anyone." Kennedy knew that with absolute certainty.

Willow shrugged. "Maybe. But that doesn't change the fact that he did it for you."

"Yeah." She glanced once more at the picture and sniffed.

Willow hugged her from the side. "You know he wouldn't want you to stay sad forever."

"I won't."

Kennedy glanced around her, and her ears soaked in the sounds of spring. The chatter of the young kids chasing after the ducklings near the ponds. The birds warbling in the trees, chirping exultantly in the glorious sunshine. Willow's phone beeping every few seconds with more texts from Nick.

She'd never known you could feel so full and so heartbroken all at the same time.

She wondered what else about life she hadn't yet discovered.

She was ready to find out.

A NOTE FROM THE AUTHOR

I can't believe Kennedy's already toward the end of her sophomore year! I want to let you know how much I appreciate you readers for making this series so exciting and enjoyable to write. I find so much inspiration knowing how many of you are waiting expectantly for Kennedy's next adventure.

Infected deals with many questions I've wondered about prayer and healing. For those of you who don't know, my family went through a very trying time after the traumatic birth of our second son. Silas stopped breathing ninety minutes after birth and suffered severe brain damage. During his first six weeks in the NICU (and his first year in and out of the hospital), we had to wrestle with many of the questions raised in *Infected*. Does God always heal people if they have enough faith? How do you know how to pray for someone who's seriously ill? Why does God chose to heal some people and not others? If you'd like to learn more about our family's personal experiences, you can read my memoir, *A Boy Named Silas.*

Infected raises a lot of questions about prayer, and if you feel like delving into some of these issues, I invite you to check out The Prevailing Prayer Podcast, a weekly show I've put together with my friend Jaime Hampton. I don't think it's a coincidence that Jaime and I were in the early stages of recording and brainstorming our first episodes of the podcast when I was working on Kennedy's most recent adventure. You can find out more or watch our most recent recordings at alanaterry.com/prayer.

As always, there are so many people to thank and acknowledge who helped me get *Infected* ready for publication. In addition to being a fabulous podcast co-host, Jaime is a great friend and prayer partner. I also want to thank my virtual buddies in the Alana & Friends group, many of whom are beta readers, early reviewers, sounding boards, and all-around cheerleaders. A special thanks to my prayer team for keeping me covered while I wrote this book.

My red-pen crew of editors and typo-slayers includes Amy, Elizabeth, Annie, Cathy, and Sandra. You are all such blessings and save me so much embarrassment. Kaye is a nurse who is always patient with my medical questions.

Last of all, I am reminded with each novel I write that I couldn't complete a single sentence without the strength and support that God provides. I'm also so grateful for the encouragement I constantly receive from my family.

DISCUSSION QUESTIONS

For group discussion or personal reflection

Are you interested in reading *Infected* or any other Alana Terry novels with a book club? Contact me at alanaterry.com for information on discounted bulk orders or to try to set up a Skype meeting with your group.

Ice Breaker Questions

1. What is the sickest you've been?

2. What are the biggest epidemics you remember living through? Did you or anyone you know get infected?

3. Do you have a favorite book or movie that deals with epidemics or hospital lockdowns?

4. Do you tend to be more like Kennedy's dad (paranoid about any possible crisis) or Kennedy (oblivious until it actually impacts you)?

5. If you were a professor, what movies or books would

you include in Kennedy's film as literature class?

6. What book would you love to see turned into a movie?

7. What's one of the strangest or most random prayers you've ever prayed?

8. When have you seen a direct answer to one of your prayers?

9. What is your favorite hymn?

10. What is a Bible verse that encouraged you during a difficult time?

Story-Related Questions

1. When you pray for somebody who is seriously ill, how do you know what to say?

2. Do you have strong opinions on the use of quarantine measures to stop the potential spread of disease? Does this feel like a wise precaution or a limitation of personal liberties?

3. Have you heard of any court cases like the one mentioned here? In this instance, which side would you take?

4. Many people dislike hospitals. What's your least favorite hospital experience you're willing to talk about?

5. What are some of the questions you had (or have) as a new believer?

6. What are some of the questions you have about faith,

prayer, and healing?

7. When was a time you had to learn to accept disappointment when God didn't answer your prayer?

8. If you could ask God any one question about prayer, what would it be?

Books by Alana Terry

North Korea Christian Suspense Novels

The Beloved Daughter

Slave Again

Torn Asunder

Flower Swallow

Kennedy Stern Christian Suspense Series

Unplanned

Paralyzed

Policed

Straightened

Turbulence

Infected

See a full list at www.alanaterry.com

Made in the USA
Columbia, SC
18 September 2023

23054556R00155